NOVEMBER

GALES

Dan Bomkamp

Lovstad Publishing
Poynette, Wisconsin

ISBN: 0692490612
ISBN-13: 978-0692490617
Previous ISBN: 0615884229

Printed in the United States of America

Cover design by
Lovstad Publishing

This book is dedicated to my good friend Doug Stamm. How far we've come from those days of fishing and exploring the river bottoms as kids.

Other books by Dan Bomkamp

Adventures of Thunderfoot
More Adventures of Thunderfoot
Thanks, Thunderfoot
The Best of Thunderfoot
The Gosey
Big Edna
Voyageur
Lost Flight
Tag
Whiteout
Spirit
The Lost Treasure of Bogus Bluff

Acknowledgements

I want to thank my long time friend Doug Stamm for the information he gave me about the lake trout project and the underwater scenes in this book. We grew up together in and on the Wisconsin River and its backwaters and we both have had a love of the outdoors ever since.

I also want to thank my publisher and friend Joel Lovstad. We spend a lot of time together at book shows and that time is always enjoyable. I apologize for the OK's.

Lastly I want to thank the many people who read my books. When I work hundreds of hours to write a book it's great to see that people enjoy them. I'm especially happy to see young people reading them. Nothing makes me happier than to see a kid with an armful of my books.

NOVEMBER

GALES

Chapter 1

I took the picture from the top of the dresser and wiped the dust from the frame onto the tail of my shirt. It was the last thing I had to pack; I stopped to look at it. I had to smile at the look on our faces. A stranger at the lighthouse overlook had taken it for us.

We saw the lighthouse on the shore of Lake Superior and pulled into the wayside looking in awe at the huge lake. Mark and I got out of the car and looked over the rock wall at the biggest lake we'd ever seen.

"We should have that guy take a picture." Mark's voice came into my head.

"Good idea." I replied in kind.

Mark walked over to the tourist and asked him if he'd take a picture and he was happy to do so. We climbed up on the rock wall with our backs to Lake Superior and hammed it up for the camera. Mark, my twin brother was on the left with one arm around my shoulder and the other held out wide like he was trying to embrace the whole world. I had my arm around his shoulder and was mimicking his pose. As many times as I'd seen pictures of Mark and me, this one still made me smile. We'd grown up like most identical twins, wearing the same clothes and getting the same haircuts. When we went to college we stopped dressing alike but it was uncanny; we still ended up most days wearing the same things. I'd get up and shower and dress and when Mark came into the kitchen of our rented apartment, he'd be wearing the same color shirt and same kind of pants or shorts. We've worn our hair fairly long as is the style with guys our age and that along with a pretty solid six foot frame doesn't hurt if we meet some girls we like. I wouldn't say we we're drop dead gorgeous but we've never had any problem picking up girls.

We grew up along the Wisconsin River in South West Wisconsin and have fished and hunted all of our lives. We've always been interested in building things and that has taken us to college where we're majoring in structural engineering. We hope one day to design and build boats and ships.

Growing up we'd gotten used to communicating without speaking. We'd be doing something and I'd know what Mark was thinking without him saying it. He did the same with me. We'd react without saying anything. I guess we never really thought much about it. Actually we thought everyone did exactly the same thing until we got into middle school. No one ever asked us about knowing what the other was thinking so we just figured everyone did the same thing with a brother or sister. Then we found out that what we had was a "twin thing". There was another set of identical twins in our school and in talking to them one day they mentioned communicating without talking and we said we did it all the time. It did make sense since neither of us had ever heard thoughts from anyone else.

They explained that they were told it was because we'd once been a single fertilized egg that had split into two identical people. Somehow being wired exactly alike we could "hear" what each other thought. We never thought much about it and just got used to doing it without making a big deal of the gift.

In the picture we had huge smiles on our faces anticipating a summer of adventure on the Great Lakes. It seemed like yesterday that the picture had been taken but it was actually over five months earlier when we had set out to find jobs on one of the ships on the big lakes.

Mark was driving as we came over the crest of the hill and saw Lake Superior for the first time.

"Holy smokes, will you look at that?" he said pulling over to the side of the highway.

"There's a place to stop up ahead," I said. "Look at that lighthouse, let's pull in there and get a picture."

Mark pulled off onto the lookout point and we got out and walked over to the rock wall that kept people from toppling down the side of the hill. There was a big boulder by the wall with a bronze plaque fixed to it. I began to read:

> Lake Superior is the largest of the Great Lakes bounded on the north by the Canadian Province of Ontario and on the south by the states of Minnesota, Wisconsin and Michigan. It is the Largest freshwater lake in the world with a surface area of 31,700 square miles. The average depth is 483 feet with a maximum depth of 1,332 feet. The shoreline of Lake Superior is 2,726 miles. There is enough water in Lake Superior to cover the entire landmass of North America and South America to a depth of 1 foot.

"Holy smokes," Mark said. "Are you sure we want to get a job on a boat on that lake?"

"It's kind of intimidating isn't it? I said. "But we want to get some practical training to be engineers. There's no better place than on a huge ship. If we want to design boats, this is the place to learn about how they work."

"Yeah, you're right," he said, "but this is a pretty darn big lake. We're used to the Wisconsin River and a few little ponds. Do you think it's safe for us to go out onto that?"

"People do it every day Mark," I said. "Look I can see three, wait, no, four big ships out there right now. It's got to be pretty safe or they wouldn't get people to work on those ships would they?"

"I guess you're right. And I guess learning about ships and

how they're built by working on one is a much better way to understand the engineering of them than reading about it in a book."

When we'd had our picture taken we thanked the man and I said, "Well, let's go down this road and see what we can find in the harbor at Superior."

The highway wound down the hill and soon we were driving down the main street of Superior, Wisconsin. On the right there were docks where many big ships were tied up loading or unloading goods. The ships were huge up close. Many of them were tied up near giant silos and were being filled with grain or corn. As we made the turn at the end of the street we saw the main harbor and were amazed at how many huge ocean-going ships were in the harbor either being loaded or unloaded.

"Jeez, look at the size of these things," Mark said. "Some of them are two football fields long."

"I know, you don't realize how big they are until you get this close to them."

"What do you think we should do? I doubt that there is a place like an employment office. I wonder if we should just go to a ship and ask about a job?"

I shrugged. "I guess we can try it and if that doesn't work we'll think of something else.

We drove down the street and saw three huge ships that were tied up getting loaded with some kind of grain. Mark turned onto a road that led down to the docks and we pulled up next to a bunch of cars and pickups in a little gravel parking lot. We got out and walked down the dike to the first ship.

There were big tubes extending from giant silos and they were pumping what looked like wheat into the holds of the ship. There were sailors here and there on the ship and we saw one young guy coming down the walkway. We walked over to him.

"Hi," I said, "Is there someone we can talk to about working?"

He looked at us strangely.

"You look work?"

"Yes we want to find jobs on a ship."

"I, not good English, but little."

"Do you know if there are jobs?" Mark asked.

"Jobs on ship here?" he said pointing up at the ship.

We nodded.

"This ship go USSR. Fill with grain then go St. Petersburg."

"Oh wow, we never thought of that," I said.

"Are there any of these ships that don't go to other countries?"

"Like stay Great Lakes?"

"Yeah, some that stay here in USA."

"Some do, not here. These ships all go Europe, Asia," he said pointing to the other two ships.

"Okay, thank you."

"Welcome. Good luck find job."

We turned around and walked back to the car.

"Well that changes things. I never thought about the fact that some of these ships leave the US and go across the ocean. I don't think we want a job on a ship going to someplace in Europe."

"Well we'll have to ask around and see if there are some that just stay here," I said.

We got back on the main road and drove farther into the harbor. Many of the ships were tied up near silos and it looked like they were being filled with grain or corn. We drove deeper into the harbor and saw a ship being loaded with scrap iron.

"I doubt if that one is going to the ocean," I said.

We found the road that led to the dock and walked down by the ship. There was a big crane with a grabber on it snatching scrap iron out of a barge and dumping it into the holds of the ship.

"There's a guy," Mark said pointing down the dock.

The guy was talking on a phone that had a line coming off the ship. We walked up to him.

"Okay, have them bring the next barge up in half an hour, this one is nearly empty."

"Hello, are you from this ship?" I asked.

"I'm the second officer," he said.

"My brother and I are studying engineering and are looking to work on ship for the summer to get some practical knowledge of engineering. We hope to design and build ships and boats someday."

"We were wondering if you might have any jobs?"

"We're looking for an electrician," the guy said.

"Hmm, we're not electricians. You don't have anything for just unskilled labor?"

"Sorry, not right now."

"Any idea if some other ship might need someone?"

"I'd check around in the upper harbor. Most of the ships there stay on the Great Lakes. The ones by the grain docks are international ships."

We thanked him and walked back to the car feeling kind of let down.

"Well this might have been a bad idea," I said.

It was getting late in the afternoon so we decided to start fresh the next day. We stopped at a drive-in and had some burgers and asked the waitress if there was a campground anywhere nearby. She gave us directions and we drove out of town a few miles to a little campground and paid $5 for a campsite. Since we didn't have a tent our plan was to sleep in the car.

"Well tomorrow might be a better day," I said poking a stick into our campfire. We had parked the car in the place where a tent usually would sit and were sitting at our picnic table staring into a campfire we'd built.

"All we can do is try," Mark said.

"You don't sound very enthusiastic," I said.

Mark grinned. "I guess I thought we'd just sashay up and some ship would be thrilled to have us for the summer. I didn't think about international ships and trained sailors."

"Well, don't give up yet, this is just our first day," I said.

In a little while we were both yawning so we got into the car. Mark got in the back seat and I tried to get comfortable in the front. We took off our shoes and tried to stretch out. The steering wheel was in the way of my knees so I couldn't stretch out but I tried to make do. We had a couple of blankets from the trunk but didn't need them.

"Dang it's hot and stuffy in here," Mark said.

"Let's open a couple of windows a little so we get some fresh air."

We cranked down each window a few inches and soon had a nice breeze going through the car.

Chapter 2

I was in that place where you find yourself when you're starting to wake up but aren't really awake yet. I could hear a humming sound and my brain was trying to figure out what it was. My legs were cramped up and my back ached from the lumpy car seat. Then I felt a sharp jab on my cheek and swatted a mosquito. I opened my eyes and blinked and then sat up.

"Holy crap, the car is full of mosquitoes," I said loudly.

Mark sat up in the back seat and looked confused.

"What the, where are we?"

"We're camping remember?"

"Damn look at all the mosquitoes," he said swatting a bunch of them on his arms and face.

Mosquitoes rose up in the car like a black cloud. The humming sound increased now that more of them were flying rather than sucking blood from Mark and me.

We got out of the car and realized we'd made a big mistake by opening the windows. The car was full of mosquitoes and they'd been feeding on us all night long.

"Holy crap, I'm full of bites," I said.

We were both scratching and swatting more mosquitoes.

"Let's get the heck out of here," Mark said.

We got in the car and opened the windows and drove out to the highway. After a couple of miles with the windows open the car was free of the little bloodsuckers.

"Well that was a fine idea," I said grinning at my brother.

"No more car camping," he said.

We stopped at a restaurant and had breakfast. I went to the bathroom and when I saw myself in the mirror I looked pretty tough.

"We need a shower and a change of clothes," I said. "We look like we slept in a car for the last month. We'll never find a job looking like bums."

"We've got clean clothes, but where can we shower?"

"There's a lake, why can't we go down to the beach and wash up?

I shrugged. "I guess that would work."

We found a park that had a nice sand beach. There was no one in the park so early in the morning so we stripped down to our boxers and sprinted to the water carrying a bar of soap and a bottle of shampoo. We tossed our towels on the sand and waded into the water.

"Holy Hanna," Mark gasped.

"Jeez that water is like ice," I said as the water rose up to just below my crotch.

"Oh man," Mark said splashing water on his body.

"As much as I hate to do it, I think if we just go all the way under we'll get it over with quicker," I said.

We both got wet and then washed with the soap. We washed inside our boxers and then we got our hair wet and shampooed it and then took a deep breath and submerged to rinse off.

Mark came up like a whale breaching.

"I'm clean enough," he said through chattering teeth.

We ran from the water and grabbed our towels. Then we ran to some bushes and stripped off our boxers and dried off and then put on dry boxers. Next we sprinted to the car and dressed in clean clothes.

We were still chilled but smelled a lot better and looked a lot better too.

"Well, let's try some more ships," I said.

We spent the day going from ship to ship and didn't even come close to finding a job. There were a couple of them that were hiring but wanted experienced sailors or something like a mechanic or radioman.

By late afternoon we were pretty discouraged.

"Maybe we'll have to forget about a job on a ship," Mark said.

"Let's give it one more day."

"I'm not sleeping in the car again," he said.

"We can't afford a motel room."

"Maybe we can find a cheap tent or a real cheap motel."

We drove along and saw a couple of guys fishing off a dock. We stopped and walked over and asked them about a cheap motel or someplace to buy a cheap tent.

"There's an Army Surplus Store a few blocks from here," one said. "They've got some old surplus tents that don't cost much."

We thanked him for the information and got directions.

"Look, there's the Army Surplus Store," Mark said, "let's see if they have a cheap tent."

We stopped at the store and went inside. There were a lot of tents to choose from. There were some real nice nylon ones that were way too expensive and some surplus pup tents that were left over from WWI or Korea. They were only $8 so we bought one and a couple of cheap air mattresses.

We stopped at a drive-in and ate and asked about a place to sleep where there weren't so many mosquitoes. The waitress suggested we sleep on the beach at the park down the road. She said it wasn't a campground but that the city didn't mind if people stayed a day or two in tents.

We found the place and pitched the tent on the dry sand. Just before dark we gathered a bunch of driftwood and made a campfire.

"What do you think?" Mark asked as we sat in the sand barefoot looking into the fire.

"About a job?"

"Yeah, it doesn't look good."

"I guess we should have thought this out a little better. I thought we could come up here and find work pretty easy. I guess I was wrong."

"We forgot about that "experience" factor."

"Yeah and how do you get experience when no one will hire you without experience?"

While the air mattresses and the tent weren't luxurious they were much better than trying to sleep in a car. I fell asleep quickly and woke some time later when Mark shook me awake.

"Hear that?"

"Hear what?"

Just then the sky flashed and a huge clap of thunder came from the west. Within a second another flash of lightning brightened the sky and more thunder sounded.

"Uh oh," I said.

"You think this tent is waterproof?" Mark asked.

"I think it probably was when it was made... in the 1940's. I guess we'll see if it still is."

We both lay there awake and soon the sound of raindrops began to come from the tent above us. At first it was just a sprinkle but in a minute it turned to a downpour.

Mark turned on the flashlight we'd brought from the glove compartment and shined it on the roof of the tent.

"It looks okay so far," he said.

The storm got louder and more lightning and thunder sounded through the darkness. Mark turned on the flashlight again and the tent looked darker.

"I think it's getting saturated with water," I said.

"Does it seem like it's lower?" Mark asked.

It did indeed seem like there was less space above us than there had been. The material on the sides was very close to touching our sleeping bags.

"We better scoot over to the middle," I said. "They say if you touch a wet tent from the inside it will leak."

We moved as close to the middle as we could. The storm raged on. After a few minutes the rain let up a bit and in another few minutes it was just a sprinkle again.

"I think it's over," I said.

Mark turned on the flashlight and shined it on the tent and the material looked very wet.

"Whatever you do, don't touch it," he said.

"Try not to roll to the side," I said.

Mark turned off the light and we lay next to each other in the darkness.

"Mike?" Mark said.

"Yeah?"

"What are we going to do if we don't find a job on a ship?"

"I don't know. I hate to go home looking like a couple of losers. We could look for some other kind of work up here."

"Yeah, I suppose. I'm getting kind of discouraged. It's like maybe it's a sign that we shouldn't be on a ship."

"Oh don't give up yet, we'll find something."

"Okay, good night, love ya bro."

"Me too."

We woke to the sound of an air horn and looked out of the tent to see a huge ship heading out of the harbor just barely visible in a dense fog. There was a slight breeze coming off the lake and it was chilly to say the least.

"Well, time for a bath?"

"Oh man, I think I'd rather stink," Mark said.

"Oh come on. Don't be a baby."

We repeated our lake bath and it wasn't any warmer the second time but it didn't seem quite as bad as the first time. When we were dressed and had the place cleaned up we got into the car.

We drove for a while along the harbor and then came to the road that led across the bridge to Duluth, Minnesota on the other side of the harbor.

"Should we go across?" Mark asked.

I shrugged. "Might as well, then we can say we were in Minnesota too."

Mark turned onto the four-lane bridge. It went up a steep incline until we were several hundred feet over the harbor. Once we got to the top the road leveled off just like a highway and took us high above the ships and boats below. On the other end we went down a steep grade and were suddenly in Duluth.

We spent the entire day going from dock to dock and asking about jobs and ended up with nothing. Every time we were told there was no work we felt even more disappointed. We might have to go back home and help make hay or work in some summer job if this didn't work out.

"What do you think?" I asked Mark.

"I don't know. I sure hate to give up but it doesn't look good. These people are looking for guys who know what to do on a ship. The only ship we've ever been on is our flat bottom boat at home."

"Well, should we give up?"

"Let's give it one more day. There are still some ships we haven't tried. If we don't find something by the end of the day tomorrow we can head home."

"Ok, so what now?" I asked.

"There's a café over there," Mark said. "I'm getting pretty hungry, how about we stop and have something to eat and then see if we can go and sleep in our tent again."

"That sounds like a plan to me. I'm getting hungry myself," I answered.

We pulled into the parking lot and got out of the car. The air was cool and damp coming off the lake and it had a smell that we hadn't noticed before.

"Kinda smells... oceany," I said.

Mark laughed. "I'm not sure oceany is a word but I know what you mean. It smells a lot different than rural Wisconsin and the pigs and cows. It's fishier smelling here."

"Well, I smell some food coming from that café, so let's go in and eat."

Chapter 3

We walked into the café and sat in a booth that looked out over the harbor. There were menus on the table and we each picked one up and began to look through them.

"So how are you two handsome guys today?

We looked up to see a lady who was probably in her 40's standing by the booth with an order pad in her hand. She was a typical diner waitress in a red-checkered uniform with a solid red apron and a little cap on her head. Her hair was up in a bun and she was chewing energetically on a wad of gum.

"Oh my, you two must be brothers, maybe twins?" she said.

"Yes we're twins," I said. "I'm Mike and this is Mark, and he's fourteen minutes older than I am."

"Well you are two fine looking guys. I've always had fantasies about partying with twins," she said raising her eyebrows.

"Oh, um, yeah," Mark stuttered while his face turned bright red.

"We both have girlfriends at home and we promised them we'd be faithful," I lied, "but if we hadn't we'd sure be happy to party with a hot lady like you."

The waitress grinned. "You're just too sweet. I know I'm too old for you, but it's nice of you to make me feel like you'd be interested. So, what'll you have today?"

The daily special was a walleye dinner with all the trimmings so we both ordered that and the waitress sashayed off to the kitchen.

"Holy smokes," Mark said watching her go.

I laughed. "I bet she does that to every guy who comes in here. She probably gets twice as much in tips just by flirting."

We sat waiting for our food and looking out at the harbor.

There was a huge ocean-going ship coming into the harbor. As it got closer I read the name on the side.

"The *Olympic Rover*," I said.

"That's one of Aristotle Onassis' ships," a voice said behind me.

I turned and two guys about our age had taken a table just a short way from us while we were watching the harbor. The one that spoke was a big guy, maybe six foot three and built like a linebacker. He had a smile on his face and piercing blue eyes that looked very friendly. The other guy was smaller, around five foot nine and built more like a wrestler. His hair was blond and he had brown eyes. Both of them were good looking friendly acting guys.

"All of his ships are Olympic something or other," the other guy said.

"The guy who married Jackie Kennedy?" Mark asked.

"Yup, the very one," the guy said.

"So that ship came across the ocean," I said.

The first guy nodded. "There are lots of ships from Europe and Asia here, they come and go all the time."

"Do you guys live here?" I asked thinking they must be local since they seemed to know a lot about the area."

"We're mates on the *Edmund Fitzgerald* and we're in port for a few days. We have a room here in Duluth. Actually we have rooms in several port towns and use them when we lay over in that port. There are seven of us who share the rent and the rooms. Some are on other boats so it's seldom that all of us are in one port together or it'd get pretty crowded."

"Otherwise we'd have to get a motel room when we have a layover, and that would be a lot more expensive," the second guy said.

"I'm Mike," I said "and this is my brother Mark."

The first guy got up and shook hands with us. "I'm Thomas, and this is Paul," he said. We all shook hands and we scooted over so they could sit down in our booth.

"So you work on a boat?" Mark asked.

"We work on the biggest boat on the great lakes. Haven't you heard of the *Edmund Fitzgerald*?"

We both shook our heads. "We're from southern Wisconsin and a big boat there is a sixteen foot bass boat."

They laughed. "The *Big Fitz* is a bit bigger than that," Thomas said. "She's 729 feet long and 75 feet wide."

"Holy smokes, that's two and a half football fields long," I said. "Why did they make it an odd number like 729?"

"The locks at the St. Lawrence Seaway are 730 feet long. They allow ships to travel from the lower Great Lakes to the ocean. They built the *Fitzgerald* one foot shorter than the locks. Otherwise she wouldn't be able to leave the Great Lakes if she had a cargo for somewhere across the ocean."

Just then the waitress arrived with our food. "Oh my some more handsome boys have joined us. Thomas, Paul are you two off for a few days?" she cooed.

Thomas and Paul grinned at her. "Agnes, you've tried that old 'I've fantasized about partying with a couple of sailors' with us already... remember?"

Agnes grinned. "Never hurts to try again," she said. "What'll you guys have?"

They looked at our plates. "That looks good to me," Thomas said.

"I'll have it too," Paul said.

She put a little extra into her sway as she walked away. Paul shook his head.

"You know what's crazy? I don't think she's kidding."

We all had a good laugh and Mark and I dug into our food while our new friends talked about their adventures on the *Big Fitz*.

Chapter 4

"So what do you guys do on the boat?" Mark asked.

"It's a ship... don't call it a boat or the captain will throw you overboard. They're kind of touchy about that. We don't care if you call it a boat but be careful and don't say it to the old guys," Paul said. "I'm a deck hand. When we're loading ore onboard I help with that and then help putting the cargo hold covers on and tightening them down. During the voyage I check that everything is tight and as it should be and do whatever the engineer or captain tells me to do. Sometimes I end up in the galley peeling potatoes, sometimes I'm a waiter... it just depends."

"I'm an oiler," Thomas said. "I work in the engine room keeping the engines running and oiling things that need oiling. The engine is an 8,000 horsepower Westinghouse Engine that moves the ship. There is also a 400kilowatt turbine generator that powers all of the electrical needs of the ship. It takes a lot of maintenance to keep them running in tip-top shape... a lot of parts and pieces to oil, so that's what my job is... an oiler."

"So you're a trained mechanic then?" I asked.

"Oh no, I'm in my senior year at the University of Wisconsin," Thomas said. "I've been working on the *Fitzgerald* the last two summers. I started out as a wiper. That's a job that also takes part in the engine room. A wiper wipes up oil and other messes from the engines. Now I make the mess, and somebody else wipes it up."

"That's what we're doing here," Mark said. "We're both engineering students at UW Platteville. We have been taking a lot of courses in structural engineering and are hoping to be able to build boats and ships someday. We thought that getting a job on a boat, oops, I mean ship would be a good way to get some practical knowledge that we could use with our book-learning."

Agnes arrived with our new friends' meals and then refilled our drinks.

"Anything else hun?" she said winking at Mark.

He grinned, "We'll let you know on that."

Agnes cackled with laughter as she swung her hips back and forth back to the kitchen.

"Jeez, don't encourage her," Thomas said.

"So you guys are looking for work on a ship," Paul said.

"Yeah, do you have any suggestions?" I replied.

Paul looked at Thomas. "Isn't that guy from Toledo planning on leaving?"

Thomas nodded. "Yeah I think he said he had a job closer to home on a ship on Lake Erie."

"The captain will probably be off the ship for the next couple of days. We're going to load up again on Friday and take a load of taconite to Detroit. You guys should see if you might be able to get a job on *The Fitz.*"

"Wow, that'd be super. Nothing could be better than being on the biggest ship on the great lakes. We'll have to find a place to camp or find a cheap motel though," I said.

Thomas looked at Paul and he nodded. "Why not come to our place? It's not fancy, in fact it's kind of a dump but we've got plenty of beds and a roof over our head. It's all paid for so there's no need for you to spend your money on a motel. It'd be much better to spend a bit of it on some cold malt beverages." He was grinning as he nodded his head.

"This could be a lucky break for us."

"No kidding, this is just what we were looking for."

I looked at Mark. "That sounds like a good idea to me, what do you think?"

"This fish is a bit salty. I'm getting a little parched. How far is this room and is there a beer store near?"

"Close on both accounts," Paul said.

We finished up our meal and left a nice tip for Agnes. She

urged us to come back soon and we walked out into the parking lot.

"That's our car," I said pointing to Mark's and my 1970 Chevy sitting a short way away.

"Cool, we don't have a car here. Let's go and we can stop on the way and get a little refreshment," Thomas said.

We loaded up and headed out onto the main street with our two new friends. We sure had gotten lucky picking this café to stop at and it might just lead to the job we had been looking for. Things were looking good.

Chapter 5

We only drove three blocks and there was a beer and liquor store on the corner.

"Are you guys 21?" Thomas asked.

"No, we're 20, aren't either of you 21?"

"Both of us are," Paul said. "I'm 22 and Thomas is 23, so we're good."

We walked into the beer store and Thomas picked up a 24 pack of St. Paulie Girl beer. Mark grabbed a couple of bags of chips and I got a chunk of cheese and a box of crackers and we put it all on the counter. The lady behind the counter packed the food into a bag and I handed her a twenty-dollar bill.

"Are you 21 son?" she asked.

"They both are," I said nodding to Thomas and Paul. I handed Thomas the $20 and he paid just to make it legal.

Thomas showed her his ID and she rang up the purchase and off we went.

"Our place is just down the block on the left," Paul said pointing to a nondescript gray building. It was an old two-story house with a stairs going up the side to the top floor. There was a parking space behind the building so we pulled in and parked the car.

"We've got half of the top floor," Thomas said.

We all trouped up the stairs and went into a narrow hallway that divided the front half from the back. Thomas went to the door on the left and opened it with a key and we walked in. To say it was kind of dump wasn't an exaggeration. The place consisted of one big room, a walk-in closet and a bathroom. There was a kitchenette on the right that had a small refrigerator, a stove and a sink. There was a metal cupboard standing next to the refrigerator. Other than that there was an old kitchen table, six mismatched wooden chairs and two sets of single bed bunk beds. There was an old dresser and an old TV stood on a crate that used to contain oranges.

"Welcome to Chez-Dump," Thomas said sweeping his arm across the room.

"*What a dump!*"

"*It's better than sleeping in the car or in the tent.*"

"*Yeah you've got that right.*"

"*And I bet the shower is a lot warmer than the lake.*"

"*I'm sold.*"

"It's very... homey," Mark said grinning.

"I told you it was a dump, but it's cheap and we're only here now and then. The other guys we share it with come and go too, and basically it's a place to sleep, shower and wait for our next trip to sea."

Paul put the beer in the refrigerator and the snacks on the table. I noticed a couple of bowls on the floor next to the sink and a flat plastic box filled with some kind of grit.

"Do you have a dog?" I asked.

"No, we have a cat, but she's stand-offish with strangers. She's probably hiding in the closet or bathroom. Once you're here for a while she'll sneak out and check you out.

"Who takes care of her when you're all gone?" I asked.

"Cats can take care of themselves. We leave her food and water dish full and she poops and pees in the litter box. Cats don't need people. They make their own fun and seem to be just fine sitting on top of a refrigerator or bed watching us like she's studying us. It's not often that nobody is here though, so usually she's only here for a day or so alone."

"Who owns the cat?" Mark asked.

Paul looked at Thomas. "Well, we'd been feeding this other cat we named Margaret. She was a stray and we saw her trying to catch a bird by the neighbor's birdfeeder one day, so we felt sorry for her and started putting out food for her. She'd come and eat but she wouldn't let us touch her. Then she was gone for a while and one day she showed up and there was this little tiny gray tiger kitten with her. One of the guys started putting out bowls of milk for the kitten and it didn't take long and the darn little thing was sitting on his lap purring up a storm."

Thomas cut in, "Then one day Margaret vanished. She stopped showing up for her food but the kitten was still hanging around. One of the guys named her Tigger and soon she'd follow us up the steps and come into the house with us. Then one evening last fall we had the windows open and were watching TV and we heard this scratching on the window there by the kitchen and there was Tigger hanging onto the screen looking in at us."

"I walked down the street to a grocery store and bought a pan and a bag of cat litter and she's been here ever since. I guess she decided that she'd allow us to provide for her and feed her," Paul said laughing.

"We've never had a cat," Mark said.

"Our mom didn't like them but we've had dogs all our lives." I said.

"Well one of these times you'll look up and there will be Tigger studying you," Paul said. "If she approves she'll come and sit on your lap, if not, leave her alone, she'll claw you and it hurts like heck."

Mark and I laughed. "I think Tigger runs this place," I said.

"You know you're right. Funny isn't it? A little critter like that can get humans to do whatever she wants with hardly any effort."

"Yeah a bunch of big tough sailors are servants to a stray cat," I said.

"So," Paul said, "anyone for a fermented malt beverage?"

Chapter 6

The 24 pack of beer was gone and we all were a little silly a few hours later. It was nearly 1:00 AM and it's a good thing we'd only bought one case of beer or we'd have probably been up all night. We were having a good time playing penny-anti poker and getting to know our new friends. We'd inhaled all of the snacks along with the beer so when all of the food and drink were gone it seemed like a good idea to go to bed.

"There are sheets and blankets in that dresser," Thomas said. "Pillows are on the beds."

Mark and I made up two beds while Thomas and Paul went to the bathroom. Mark used the facilities next and then I took my turn. When I came back into the living/bedroom, everyone was already bedded down. I turned off the light and crawled into the lower bunk below Mark.

"Goodnight all," Paul said.

A chorus of "goodnights" answered him. Within three minutes Thomas was snoring like a chainsaw.

"Holy smokes," Mark whispered. "Remind me to buy some earplugs tomorrow."

I laughed. "He's a heavy sleeper it seems."

I lay there on my back thinking how lucky we'd been to meet these guys. We could easily be sleeping in the car at some wayside and here we were in comfy beds with a roof over our heads after an enjoyable evening with two new friends. I closed my eyes and let a sigh and suddenly I felt a slight movement on the bed. I opened my eyes and there was the cat lying on my chest looking into my eyes.

"Well hello," I whispered. "You must be Tigger."

At the mention of her name the cat's eyes blinked. She leaned forward and smelled my nose and then her rough little tongue came out and she licked the tip of it.

"Meow," she said quietly.

"So, do I pass" I asked.

She snuggled down on my chest and I heard her start to purr. She rubbed her face across my neck a couple of times and soon she was silent and not moving.

"Hmm, well I guess she's okay with me," I thought to myself.

I closed my eyes and it felt nice to feel the soft little body on my chest and feel her breathing. I fell asleep in no time.

"So it looks like Tigger likes you," Mark said leaning down over the top bunk.

I opened my eyes. It was bright and sunny outside and the sunlight was streaming in through the window. I looked down and there was Tigger still lying on my chest but looking up at Mark. She looked at him and then at me and then she looked back at him.

I laughed. "I think she's confused seeing two of the same person."

Thomas rolled over and farted. "There's a morning kiss for my new roommates."

Tigger heard the fart and ran off toward the closet.

"Jeez you scared the cat," I said.

Paul groaned. "Better get ready to evacuate the room," he said. "Thomas' beer farts are like toxic waste."

Mark and I were laughing when the smell hit us. "Holy smokes," Mark gasped.

He jumped down from the top bunk in his boxers and I climbed out of my bunk. Paul was already opening the windows and we followed him out into the hallway and then to the stairs outside.

He left the door open letting a breeze flow through the hallway. "That breeze should clear it out pretty fast," he said shivering in the cool damp morning air that was coming off the lake.

"Good God, is he always that stinky?" Mark asked.

"You have no idea," Paul said. "And I'm his roommate on the

Fitzgerald, I have to smell that every day."

"Poor Tigger," I said.

"You can come back now," Thomas said loudly from inside. "I went to the bathroom and vented."

Paul looked at us. "Do not... I repeat do not go in the bathroom for at least a half hour. There's a ceiling fan but it takes a long time to clear it out."

"Oh man, I gotta pee," Mark said.

"Over there," Paul said pointing to an old shed with lilac bushes planted around it. "I go there a lot when there's an emergency."

"I gotta get dressed first," Mark said.

"Don't worry, nobody'll see you, there's bushes all around here and the people downstairs are used to seeing guys in boxers peeing back there. Thomas is a legend around here."

Mark and I laughed like ten year olds as we sprinted down the steps and back behind the shed, did our business and then ran upstairs again. When we got into the apartment, we smelled bacon.

Thomas was at the stove in his boxers and a tee shirt frying bacon. "The toast'll be up in a minute. Somebody butter it and put in a couple more slices."

Mark looked at me and grinned. "I think we found the perfect guys to stay with... they're just like us."

"Boy, you got that right," I said.

Chapter 7

After breakfast we took turns taking showers and when we all were clean and dressed for the day Thomas suggested we go down to the lake and do some fishing.

"There are public docks down the street a little way where you can sit and fish for free," he said.

"We don't have any fishing poles with us," I said.

"We've got a whole bunch of them in the closet. Most of the guys who stay here just leave a pole so there's never a shortage. Sometimes we catch some nice perch off those docks. If we could catch a couple dozen we could have a fish fry tonight."

That sounded good to us so we gathered up the gear and loaded up in Mark's and my car and headed to the bait shop. We bought a couple of boxes of night crawlers and a 12 pack of cold beer just in case we got thirsty while we were fishing.

We pulled into a parking lot and followed the guys down to the lake and out onto the dock. There were small fishing boats tied up to the dock while their owners went up to have a meal or buy some groceries but there was plenty of room to fish. The dock stuck out into the lake about 200 feet.

There were several old fishermen sitting on lawn chairs fishing along the way and we greeted them all as we went past. One seemed to know Thomas and Paul and they stopped and asked him how the fishing was.

"The fishin's pretty good, but the catchin's not much," he said grinning.

Thomas took a cold beer from the 12pack and handed it to the old guy.

"Here, maybe this will help," he said.

"That it might," the old guy said, "At least I won't care as much if they bite or not. Thanks boys, I appreciate it."

We moved on toward the end of the dock.

"Kind of a cool old guy."

"Yeah he reminds me of our grandpa."

"Is he a regular?" I asked.

Paul nodded. "We've never been here when he wasn't here."

We got to the end and each took a spot and sat down with our feet hanging over the dock.

"Put your bobber up about at 6 feet," Thomas said.

We all rigged up, baited with half a crawler and tossed out our lines.

"Who's parched?" Thomas asked holding up the beer.

All three of us raised our hands. Thomas passed out three beers and then took one himself. The sound of four cans being opened made us grin.

"I could get used to this life," Mark said.

"We work pretty hard when we're out to sea but when we get on land we like to kick back and have fun," Paul said.

"So who is Edmund Fitzgerald?" I asked.

"When the ship was being built back in 1957, he was the chairman of the board of the Northwestern Mutual Life Insurance Company. Most ships are named for somebody in the company that builds them. They did their sea trials in the fall of '57 and they made their first voyage through the Soo Locks shortly after that. Actually the locks are called Sault St. Marie, because the city where they are built is the same name. Sault is pronounced Soo, so they became the Soo Locks. The captain was Captain Larson and he commanded the ship for seven years until 1966 when Captain Peter Pulcer took over."

"So it's been operating for quite a few years," I said.

"Yeah and it's had its problems. Have you ever seen how they launch a big ship like this?"

Mark and I shook our heads no.

"They're built on a dry dock and have big wooden blocks holding them upright. They look like the blocks that hold up a model ship. Then when they're christened they break a bottle of champagne over the bow. The wife of Mr. Fitzgerald had to hit the ship three times with the bottle before it broke which means bad luck. Then with 15,000 people watching they knocked the blocks out from the lower side and the ship slid off the dock, and slammed into another dock across the way. The other dock was demolished and the huge wave that was made washed about a hundred people into the lake.

Just then Mark's bobber went down. He grabbed his pole and reeled in a nice perch. "Hey, cool," he said.

My bobber went down just at that time Mark got his fish up and I began reeling. Paul's bobber disappeared and while he and I were reeling in Thomas's bobber went down. In no time we had 4 fat perch flopping on the dock. Mark had baited up again and when his line hit the water the bobber settled and went right down.

"Holy smokes, I've got another one," he said.

Then things went crazy.

Telling it takes almost longer than what happened. From then on for the next 15 minutes our bobbers would just hit the water and keep going down. Every time one of us got a line in the water we caught a big perch. We had fish flopping all over the place and some were flopping back into the water.

Thomas yelled over to the old guy on the dock, "Henry, bring your pail over here and fish with us. We have a school of perch right under us!"

Henry came scurrying down the dock and we started throwing our fish into his five-gallon bucket. He sat beside us and began catching perch after perch with us.

I'd never caught fish so fast. There must have been thousands of them under the dock. We laughed and yelled and had a fantastic time. But then after about 15 minutes the action slowed. We were still catching one now and then but the school definitely had moved through. Soon the action stopped all together.

Henry was sitting there grinning like mad. "Now that's some fun ain't it boys?"

"That was something, holy smokes, that was really something," Paul said.

I got up and looked into the bucket.

"We've got nearly a full bucket," I said.

"It looks like we're having a fish fry tonight," Thomas said.

"Henry, why don't you come up to the fish cleaning shack with us and we'll all pitch in and clean these fish. Then you can come over and have a fish fry with us and take the left over fish home. We're going out to sea on Friday so you might as well take them."

"That'd be a fine with me," Henry said. "My social calendar is pretty open just now so I think I can fit it in."

I grinned at the old guy. He reminded me of my own grandpa and I knew he was enjoying the company as much as we were.

"Well, let's load up and get these fish cleaned. We need to stop at the grocery store and probably the beer store too," Thomas said.

There were smiles all around as we hiked up the dock.

Chapter 8

The fish shanty was provided by the city as a place for fishermen to clean their catch. It was a small building with screen windows on all sides to keep the flies out and to let a lot of fresh air flow through. There was a long stainless steel countertop with a sink in one end on the side. The other side was open and had a plastic bag dispenser on the wall as well as garbage cans with tight lids for the fish heads and guts.

We dumped the pail of perch out on the counter and Thomas and Paul began to fillet them. It didn't take long to see they were not very skilled at the job. I turned to Mark and raised my eyebrows and shrugged.

"You want us to help?" Mark asked.

"Well, I thought I knew how to do this but I'm not very good," Paul said.

"We'll be here for a while I think," Thomas said.

Henry hadn't said a word but stood to the side watching. He stepped forward and took the knife from Paul's hand.

"Why don't you let me fillet them and you guys take the ribs out?"

"There won't be enough for us to do with four of us and only one of you," I said.

Henry smiled. "Watch and learn."

He took a perch, laid it on its side, cut in behind the head just to the backbone, turned his knife and sliced the fillet off the side as slick as a whistle. He stopped short of the tail, turned the fish over and repeated the operation on the other side. Then he cut the tail free releasing the two sides of the fish, connected by the tail skin.

He looked at us and said, "Now, you guys do this."

He took his knife and sliced the ribs out of the fillet, put his knife flat on the skin at the tail and pulled, stripping off the skin and leaving a boneless, skinless fillet. Then he turned the second fillet over and repeated the moves and one perch was done.

"Now two of you take the ribs out and skin them while the third guy rinses them off and bags them up. The fourth guy can get rid of the carcasses and keep me supplied in fish that need filleting."

"Any questions?" the old man asked. "Ok, let's fillet some fish boys," he said.

It was like watching an artist as Henry went through the pail of perch. He could take the fillets off fast enough that two of us couldn't keep up to him. Every now and then he'd stop and skin and de-rib some to help us catch up.

"Henry's a magician."

"No kidding we'd be here for a week."

In about twenty minutes we had the whole pail of fish finished and Paul rinsed the last two fillets and hefted the bag containing the catch.

"Wow this must be six or seven pounds of pure meat," he said.

"Henry, you da man when it comes to cleaning fish," I said.

Henry laughed. "I've cleaned many in my days boys. Once you know how, you just do it automatically. So, how about we get some fixin's and go and fry us some perch?"

Thomas hosed down the stainless steel counter and we made sure the fish house was cleaned up. Then we loaded up in the car. Henry had walked down to the pier so he rode with us. We stuck the five fishing poles out the window in the back seat and off we went. We stopped at the grocery store and picked up what Henry told us we needed and then stopped at the beer store and got a 24 pack and a 12 pack. After all Henry was probably thirsty too after all the fish cleaning.

When we got back to the room Henry went through the cupboards and found what we needed for cooking the fish. He got two large kettles out and filled each of them half full of oil and put them on the stove to heat up.

35

"Take those potatoes and wash them up and cut them into French fries," he said to Mark and me. "You guys will be responsible for the potatoes."

"Aye sir," I said.

Thomas helped Henry make some beer batter for the fish while Paul chopped up some cabbage and followed Henry's instructions to turn it into coleslaw. In no time the room smelled like a roadside tavern having a Friday night fish fry.

About twenty minutes later we had a heaping pile of fries on a platter and Henry and Thomas had a pile of golden perch fillets on another.

We all opened a cold one and sat around the table.

"To good friends and good fish," Henry said hoisting his beer up. We all touched beer cans and toasted. Then we dove into the food.

To say it was one of the best meals in my life would be an understatement. The fish was crisp and succulent, the fries were crispy and delicious and the coleslaw was a perfect accompaniment. We ate and drank and burped and just had one heck of a good time until the plates were empty.

"Holy smokes, that was the best fish I've ever eaten," Mark said.

"No kidding," Paul said. "Henry you outdid yourself."

Henry smiled and soaked up the praise.

"Thanks boys, and thanks for inviting me to fish with you and to this feast. I spend a lot of time alone now days and it's nice to have company."

"Do you live alone?" Mark asked.

"My wife died six years ago and all of my sons live all over the country, so yes, I live alone."

"You're retired?" I asked.

Henry nodded. "I was the head cook on the *Algosoo*. She was a freighter, 346 foot long and built in 1901. We were near Whitefish Point heading for Michigan on Nov. 27, 1965 and she struck a reef. We began to take on water and in no time we had a bad list to the port. The Captain ordered 'Abandon Ship' and we all set off in lifeboats in the middle of a November gale. Luckily all of us made it but the *Algosoo* went to the bottom. After that I worked on a couple of other ships but soon decided I'd been lucky enough to survive one sinking I didn't want to try a second time, so I retired and now I live on the shore. The closest I get to the lake is on the pier fishing for perch and bass."

"Wow, was it scary?" Mark asked.

"It happened so fast we really didn't have time to be scared Mark. One minute I was taking fresh bread out of the ovens for the evening meal and the next I felt a hell of a shudder when we hit the reef. Within two minutes the sirens started screaming and the captain came on the intercom and told us to get to the lifeboats. I think that was the time I was most frightened, standing there on deck, with the ship listing so badly that you had to hold onto something to keep from sliding off into the water. Once we were all in lifeboats it only took minutes for the ship to sink."

Henry paused as if reliving the scene.

"I'll tell you one thing boys, it makes you feel mighty small and vulnerable to be out in the middle of Lake Superior in the dark with ten foot waves crashing over you in November."

We all sat silently imagining the scene.

"But," Henry said grinning, "we survived and we lived on. We got lucky, many don't. There are hundreds of wrecks on the bottom of the lake boys, hundreds of them. And when a ship goes down in this lake, you're gone. Bodies are never recovered. The water is so cold that you just lie on the bottom and stay there. The Chippewa said, "When the gales of November blow, the lake never gives up her dead."

"Still want to work on a ship" Thomas said looking at Mark and me.

"We're hopefully going to be on the biggest ship on the lakes," I said, "I'd imagine she's pretty safe."

Chapter 9

We cleaned up the mess from our fish fry and Henry told us stories of the old days when he was a young seaman. We sat enthralled with his stories of close calls on the water and the adventures he had on shore.

Henry looked up to the clock and it was after midnight.

"This old sailor is up way past his bedtime," he said. "I better head for my cottage."

"Henry, I'll give you a ride," I said.

"Why don't you take the rest of the fish fillets home Henry?" Thomas said. "We're loading tomorrow and we'll be heading out late tomorrow or early Saturday. You might as well use them."

"I'll give them a good home, that's for sure," the old man said.

Henry and I walked down to the car and I drove a few blocks down along the waterfront to his cottage. It was a neat little house not far from the water.

"You guys have a safe voyage," he said as he got out.

"I'm not sure Mark and I have a job but if we do get one we'll sure have a good time," I answered.

"Just listen to the men around you and do what you're told. You'll do fine."

With that advice Henry shut the door and walked toward the building. He turned and waved as I drove out of the parking lot. I had to smile to myself. He was a pretty cool old guy.

When I got back to the room there was someone new there sitting drinking a beer with the guys.

"Here he is now," Mark said. "Mike this is Randall, he's a shareholder in this place. He just got into port."

I shook hands with the guy. He was probably in his late 20's, short, stocky and powerfully built. He nearly crushed my hand with his handshake.

"Good to meet you Mikey," he said. "I'm on the oil hauler the *Annabelle*."

We all had a nice conversation and eventually the beer ran out so we decided to go to bed.

"Wait, we're one bed short now," I said. "I'll sleep on the floor. Mike deserves a bed since he pays part of the rent for this place."

"Not to worry," Paul said. "We have extra beds."

I looked at Paul. Was he drunk? There wasn't any place to store an extra bed. The room only had the bathroom and closet and I knew there wasn't a bed in either.

"Paul went over to the closet and opened one of the doors. He returned with a flat plastic thing folded up and handed it to me.

"Here... blow," he said.

I unfolded the air mattress and began blowing it up. By the time I had it full I had a sheet and blanket to go with it. We all took turns in the bathroom and then settled down, with me on the floor between the two bunk beds.

I was just about sleeping when I felt a slight movement on my chest and opened my eyes to look up at Tigger. She was lying on my chest purring.

"Hello girl," I said. "Where have you been hiding all night?"

She leaned forward and rubbed her face against mine and then settled on her side and curled up to sleep.

It didn't take long for me to join her.

A blast from Thomas' bunk woke me several hours later. The sun was shining in the window and Paul and Mark were over by the kitchen making breakfast. Tigger was gone but Randall was snoring in the bottom bunk where I'd been before.

"Abandon ship," Mark said and he and Paul headed for the door.

I jumped up and followed them and I could hear Thomas laughing behind me.

"Come back, hey, come on back, have a courtesy sniff."

"Jeez," I said standing out on the porch landing. "You and he share a room on the ship?"

Paul shook his head. "Believe me I've tried to trade but nobody will take my room. I've even offered money and things like tape decks. He's not so bad when he's not drinking beer though. But it's a hardship, for sure."

Mark and I were laughing as Randall stumbled out onto the porch.

"Holy crap, that's horrible. He should be taken out and dropped into the deepest part of the lake."

We could hear Thomas laughing inside the room.

Chapter 10

The four of us left Randall in the room and drove to the Burlington Northern Railroad dock where the *Edmund Fitzgerald* was being loaded with taconite pellets. When we pulled up to the parking area both Mark and I sat openmouthed looking up at the giant ship.

"I can't believe something that big can float," I said. "Oh I know all about water displacement and all of that physics stuff but when you get up this close to something that big it really seems impossible that so much steel would float."

"She weighs over 13,000 tons empty," Paul said. "And she holds 26,000 tons of taconite pellets fully loaded. That's 39,000 tons."

I could tell that Mark was calculating in his head. "Oh my gosh, that's 78 million pounds? That can't be possible."

Thomas nodded. "It's possible and you're right on your calculations. She's one big old ship."

It was hard to comprehend but the physics of shipbuilding was an exact science and Mark and I were happy to be able to see how it really worked. We walked down the dock as huge elevators pumped the gray/red pellets into the ships holds.

"So what is taconite exactly?" I asked.

"Have you ever heard of the Mesabi Range" Paul asked.

"Yeah, I've heard the name, but I don't know what it is."

The Mesabi Range is an iron ore deposit in northern Minnesota in a range of mountains the Ojibwe called it the Misaabe-wajiw, or Giant's Mountain. They mine the ore, which contains about 15% iron and put it through a process where they grind it to a fine powder and then use chemicals and magnets to refine it into pellets about the size of a quarter. These are taken to the steel mills and turned into iron and steel. The Fitz can carry 26,000 tons of the stuff and that's primarily what it was built for," Paul explained.

"So that stuff pouring in is taconite?"

Paul nodded. "That's the stuff that gives us a job."

"So," Thomas said, "are you ready to go and see if we can get you a job?"

Mark and I nodded and followed them down the dock. Near the front of the ship there was a walkway suspended alongside that led up to the deck. We climbed up and stopped to look down the length of the gigantic deck.

"She's 729 feet from stern to bow, 75 feet wide and we're up 39 feet from the bottom of the ship," Paul said.

It was like nothing Mark and I had ever seen. Just then a door opened on the wheelhouse and a kid came out and smiled at Paul and Thomas.

"What? You guys can't wait to get back?" he said.

"We missed you too much Davey," Thomas said hugging the kid.

"We brought a couple of new friends," Paul said.

"Mark and Mike... this is David. He's our Cadet. He's going to the naval academy and someday will be the captain of a ship, maybe the *Fitzgerald*."

The guy shook hands with us. He was about our age, shorter than any of us and slightly built. He was very boyish looking and was wearing a uniform and a big smile.

"I'm a long way from being a captain," he said. "I've got years of training and maybe I'll end up commanding. But for now I'm the lowest grunt on the grunt list. I do all of the jobs the other officers don't want."

"He seems like a good guy."

"I think so too. He'll be a good one to become friends with."

"Davey, did the guy from Toledo leave?"

"Yeah, he left two days ago. Captain McSorley has been hoping to find a replacement but hasn't so far."

"These guys are looking for a summer job," Thomas said.

"Oh, well that might be a lucky coincidence. But I'm sure we only need one guy, not two."

I looked at Mark and we both knew that wouldn't work. We wanted to work together.

"Let's talk to the Captain and see," Paul said.

Davey led us to the wheelhouse and we followed him up some stairs to the command center of the ship. There was a young guy doing something under a cabinet with a wrench and an older man sitting looking at some papers.

"Excuse me Captain," Davey said. "Thomas and Paul would like to talk to you."

The captain looked up and smiled. "Ready for a trip?" he asked.

"Yes sir," Paul said. "We heard you lost a cook helper. Thomas and I met these two guys a couple of days ago and they're looking for a job."

The captain looked at us and then did a double take. He smiled.

"Twins!" he said.

"Yes sir, I'm Mike and this is Mark." We stepped forward and shook hands with the captain.

"Have you ever worked on a ship before?" he asked.

"No sir, we're both structural engineering students and want to someday design and build ships and boats. We thought working on a ship would be helpful for our schooling and provide an adventure."

"Well, heaven knows it'd be nice to have engineers that had knowledge of the sea. Some of the engineers design some things that are completely useless in real life. David, could we use two men?"

"Well we could Captain, but we're only budgeted for one more."

"Sir, we'd be happy to just sign up one of us and take one pay. The other will do all the same work for one salary. We'd really like to be together, it's kind of a twin thing. While we aren't rich, we've got scholarships for our schooling. So making a lot of money isn't as important as working together and learning about ships."

Captain McSorley looked at David. "What do you think?"

"I think that'd be fine sir. I'm alone in my quarters, so they both could bunk there. My room is a bit larger than a regular crew room since I'm an officer, albeit a junior officer. I have a set of bunk beds and we could put a cot in there with no trouble."

The captain looked pleased. "Is that ok with you guys?"

We both nodded and beamed with a smile. "Perfect sir... that'd be just perfect."

"And David you're sure you don't mind sharing?"

"I'd be happy for the company Sir," Davey replied.

Chapter 11

We thanked the captain and Davey walked us to the gangplank.

"So do we call you Sir?" I asked.

Davey laughed.

"No just call me Davey or David. Actually the captain is the only one who calls me David. I'm not very important. I'm just a glorified student sailor."

"Okay Davey," I said.

"We're scheduled to leave in about 5 hours. It'll take about 4 hours more to finish loading and then an hour to secure all the hatches. Why don't you guys try to be back in about 3 hours so we can get you settled and then you can start your duties?"

"We'll be here," I said.

"Is there anything special we need?" Mark asked.

"You should have some rubber soled shoes... tennis shoes are fine, and some rain gear. Otherwise anything you'd wear on shore is fine here. Do you have any clothes that are alike?" he asked.

"Yeah, some, we don't dress alike any more but often when we buy clothes we find that we both bought the same things. I guess since we have the same identical DNA we're wired alike. We seem to be able to know what each other is thinking a lot of times too. We don't really try to read the other's thoughts but suddenly I know what Mark is thinking or he knows what I'm thinking. I guess it's a special bond that twins have. Why do you ask about the clothes?"

Davey grinned. "I'm thinking we can have some fun with the crew for a while as long at they think there is just one new guy and not two identical ones."

We all grinned at that.

"Oh I can definitely see the possibilities of that," Thomas said.

We walked back to the car. On the way I asked Thomas and

Paul if there was a shop in town that sold proper rain gear and they guided us to the shop. We also bought a few extra tee shirts and underwear. The guys suggested we get a duffle bag rather than using our suitcases. While the rooms on the *Fitzgerald* were spacious compared to most freighters, there still wasn't a lot of free space. A duffle bag could be rolled up and stored in much less space than a suitcase. Mark and I each bought one.

We went back to Chez-Dump and packed our clothes. Randall was watching TV and we chatted with him while we packed.

"Where's the cat?" I asked him.

"I haven't seen her for a while. I'd look in the closet."

I walked into the closet and searched. Finally I found her in a box that contained some clothes left by someone previously.

"Hey Tigger," I said.

She looked up sleepily and meowed.

"We're going away for a while, you be a good girl," I said stroking her soft fur.

She licked my hand and settled back down to finish her nap.

"How long will you be here?" Thomas asked Randall.

"We're in port for three days. If no one else shows up before I leave I'll make sure her litter box is filled with clean litter and leave her enough food for several days. You guys will be back in how long?"

"It usually takes 5 days to Detroit and back. Sometimes it turns into 6 days if we have bad weather or get into port with another ship unloading. But we'll be back no longer than a week from now."

"She'll be fine," Paul said to me. "Cats can live on their own for a long time and make their own entertainment. They just allow humans to live with them so they can feed them and clean their toilets for them."

I laughed at that, because he was absolutely right on both counts.

We said farewell to Randall and walked down the stairs.

"Safe voyage," he shouted to us.

When we got back to the ship we found Davey in the wheelhouse. He was watching the loading from the glass-enclosed room.

"Okay, Thomas and Paul already have their room and know where it is. I'll take Mark and Mike down to the crew quarters and get them settled if that's okay Captain."

"Absolutely David, and welcome aboard boys. I look forward to a fine summer with you on board. David and I talked a little about the possibilities of twins and the fun we can have with the crew and guests and I think it looks like a fine summer ahead of us."

We were all smiles as we followed Davey to the crew-quarters area.

"There are two under-deck passageways for the crew to move from forward to aft. They're especially nice in bad weather or when the deck is iced. It's over 700 feet from the other end so this is a very nice feature. One passageway runs down each side of the ship. We climbed down some stairs to a hallway that was thickly carpeted with doors on either side every few feet.

"The *Fitzgerald* isn't typical when it comes to amenities for the crew and occasional guests. These rooms are crew-quarters. Each room is for two crewmembers. Each has its own tiled bathroom, curtains over the portholes and air conditioning. Believe me air conditioning is not something you find on most ships and it's very nice to have in the middle of the summer. Down at the other end is the Captain's quarters and the first mate and second mate. They are a little bigger and have the same nice furnishings. My quarters are next to the captain's and I've been bunking alone. My cabin is larger than a regular crew cabin, so there's plenty of room for both of you there."

"I expected something more... Spartan," I said.

"Believe me most ships have large cabins with six to eight

sailors to a cabin, and everyone shares one head, or bathroom to you guys."

"There are two dining rooms, one for large meals and the other for times when watches change. Watch is your time on duty, like your shift. There are also two guest cabins for the occasion when we have guests sailing with us."

"What kind of guests?" Mark asked.

"Usually they're company officials who are checking out the operation of the ship but sometimes they're people who work for the company that just need a ride to Detroit or Toledo."

We were shown into several extra rooms that held crew amenities. One was a TV room and there was a card room, a poolroom and a 24hour kitchen that had snacks and sandwiches available for the crew when they got off watch.

"Down here," he said pointing down the hall "is the galley and pantry. We have a fine cook who makes amazing meals for us. You guys are replacing one of his helpers. Since there isn't enough work for both of you all the time here, one can help in the galley and the other will work as a deck hand. You can change jobs as you like. Actually no one would ever know if you switched anyway," he said laughing.

He led us to the cabin and it was really very nice. In addition to the bunk beds he had a desk and chair and a tape deck on a shelf. Everything was bolted to the wall probably in case of bad weather.

"We'll go down to the storage room and get another bed," he said. "I'll move some of my stuff from the closet so you guys can put your stuff in there too. The head is right there through that door."

"This'll be great Davey," I said.

We hauled the bed back and set it up. Then Davey got us some linens and blankets and our room was ready. We put our clothes away and he took us to the galley to meet our new boss.

There was something cooking in the galley that smelled great as we entered. The cook was stirring a large pot on the stove.

Wearing white clothes and a chef hat he looked to be in his mid-forties and had a big smile on his face when we walked in.

"Davey, I think I need to go ashore and have my eyes checked," he said grinning. "I'm seeing double."

Davey laughed. "Alan, this is Mike and Mark, they're going to be your helpers and help out with deck hand chores too. Obviously they're twins, and we got a two-fer with them."

The cook shook hands with both of us and looked us up and down. "They look fit and reasonably intelligent. I think they'll do just fine."

"They're both engineering students," Davey said. "I think they can master peeling potatoes."

Alan roared with laughter. "Well, how about you two get each get a set of whites and we'll get started on the rest of the meal for the evening. Once these guys get the ship loaded and the hatches battened down, they'll be ready to eat like a bunch of famished pagans."

He showed us where the white cooks' clothes were stored and we each picked out a pair of pants and a white tee shirt.

Davey said he'd see us later and wished us good luck. And we began our new jobs on the *Edmund Fitzgerald.*

Chapter 12

Feeding 30 people took planning and some work but Alan had been doing it for years and had it down to a science. He decided that since the deck hands would be on deck tightening down the 21 hatch covers it would be hard to know for sure when everyone would be done with their duties. It would make sense to make a dinner that would be kept warm so latecomers would have good food as well as those who ate first.

"If you keep sailors full of good chow you'll never have a mutiny," Alan said to us. Alan wore a floppy chef hat and we both had white baseball caps. "We want to keep everything clean and feed the boys the best quality chow we can make," Alan said. "I take great pride in my food and expect you guys to do the same."

We assured him we'd do our best but weren't real experienced cooks.

"I'll show you exactly what I want done and if you do it, we'll all have a fine trip."

He took Mark to the storeroom and had him get 20 pounds of potatoes out. Then he had him wash them and then peel them and slice them into thin slices. We left Mark staring at a huge pile of potatoes but with a smile on his face.

"Mike you can help me with the bread."

Alan showed me how to measure out the right amount of flour, yeast, sugar, salt and water and how to combine them in a huge mixer to make a big blob of bread dough. Once it had risen we "punched it down" and let it rise again. When that was done he showed me how to cut it into proper sized loafs, put them into greased bread pans. Then we let them rise again.

"When those are up above the pans we'll bake them," Alan said. "Why don't you see how Mark is doing?"

Mark was nearly done with the potatoes so I helped him

finish slicing them up and we got instructions from Alan on how to add onions and chopped ham and turned them into scalloped potatoes. We put them into three huge pans for baking.

"We'll bake the bread now and when that's done it'll be time to start baking the potatoes."

"He's got this down to a science."

I nodded.

"He definitely knows what he's doing."

Soon the galley began to smell wonderful as the bread baked.

"That smell... and fresh popped popcorn... the scents of the gods," Alan said.

We set about helping Alan open some cans of corn and carrots and then he showed us how to make several pans of brownies for desert.

Above us we could feel the ship shuddering as the cranes lowered the 11foot by 48 foot hatch covers into place and the deck hands secured them with big bolts.

The afternoon slipped by very fast and soon everything was ready for the evening meal. "They'll be arriving soon, so we'll put out the food on this steam table," Alan said. "Then they can fill their plates and eat in either of the two dining rooms. There's a little clique of deck hands vs. engine room hands but really everyone gets along fine. You guys make sure everything stays full and hot and I'll keep watch over the kitchen."

"Well, now we meet the rest of our new friends."

"Let's just one of us at a time be out there, so they don't know there are two of us."

Mark had a devious grin on his face.

"You help Alan, I'll stay out here," he said.

It wasn't long and Davey showed up. "Boy is smells great down here," he said. "How did you get along with Alan?"

"Great," I said. "He's very organized and seems to know how to cook."

"He's a great cook, we're lucky to have him."

"So what's the plan now?"

Davey grinned. "I'm going to introduce everyone as they come in to eat, but I'm only telling them that they're meeting Mark."

I nodded. "Sounds like fun."

Davey looked at me. "So are you Mark?"

I shrugged. "Only my brother and I know for sure."

Chapter 13

I stayed in the galley while Mark was introduced to the crew. Not all were there at once because some were finishing up duties on deck and in the engine room. When most had filled their plates and taken seats, the captain and officers showed up. Mark was introduced to the First Mate and Second Mate.

"So is your brother hiding?" the First Mate asked quietly.

Mark nodded. "We're keeping him out of site for now."

The First Mate, a man named John who looked to be in his early 60's grinned. "We can have some fun with this," he said.

The three officers sat at the head of one of the tables, a space left for them by the crew and soon everyone was talking and laughing and eating.

"I'm in the hallway, go back to the galley for a minute and I'm going to walk through."

Mark nodded and grinned and made his way back into the galley. I'd gone to our room and changed into a blue tee shirt and when I saw Mark disappear into the galley I walked into the dining room and picked up a coffee pot.

"Would you like more coffee?" I asked the first sailor at the end of the table.

"Yes, thank... you," he said looking up and seeing me in a blue shirt. He got a frown on his face and looked confused. I went down the side of the table and filled everyone's cup and then went down the other side. By the time I was through the room was silent. Then I thought... *"Count to five and come back in."*

I put down the coffee pot and walked out into the hall.

Mark came out of the galley carrying a tray with sliced bread on it. You could have heard a pin drop.

Captain McSorley nearly choked trying not to laugh out loud.

When the crew was finished they all left and the captain stopped in the galley as he was heading back up to the wheelhouse.

"Great meal, Alan, and that stunt you two pulled... that was classic. The crew has no idea." He began laughing. "This is going to be fun until the crew figures it out."

We began cleaning up the dining room and galley. Once we had all the dishes collected we began washing.

Suddenly we felt a vibration in the deck below our feet.

"It feels like the engine is running," I said.

Alan nodded. "We'll be leaving the dock soon, on our way to Detroit."

We finished up our work and Alan told us to take a break so we changed into our regular clothes and walked up on the deck. We stayed back next to the wheelhouse so we were somewhat hidden and could keep the twin secret. Soon we saw some of the deck hands on deck. Some men on shore untied the huge ropes from their mooring posts and the deck hands pulled them onboard and secured them. Then the horn sounded on top of the wheelhouse and the ship began to move forward.

"Wow, we're really on our way out to sea," I said.

"This is very cool," Mark added.

The ship began to move slowly at first but in no time we could see that it was speeding up. The captain was turning it out into the harbor and when we were clear of the dock he gave two toots on the horn. When we got to the end of the harbor we moved out into Lake Superior and it looked vast and featureless.

"That's a lot of water," Mark said quietly.

"Pretty darn big, but I think the captain knows where he's going," I answered.

We watched the shore grow smaller and smaller until there was no shore to be seen. We were out in wide-open water and the waves were beginning to build. The ship, being so big didn't respond very much to the rough water but after a while it began to have a definite sway to it.

"Ooh, my stomach is feeling a little unsettled," Mark said.

I turned to him. He had a slight green cast to his skin.

"I think you're seasick," I said grinning.

"I think you're right," he said.

"Maybe we should go below and see if Alan needs us," I suggested.

"I think I need to... oh boy!"

Mark hurried to the rail and lost his dinner over the side. I held onto him to steady him. "Are you okay now?" I asked.

"No, please shoot me."

He was sweating and was very pale.

I laughed and helped him back down the stairs to our room. "I'll go and help Alan, you try to rest a bit," I said.

"If I'm dead when you get back just bury me at sea."

I walked down to the galley. Alan was there in the cooler writing down all the provisions we had.

"So, we're underway, how are you taking the sea?" he asked.

"I'm fine but Mark is a little under the weather."

Alan laughed. "I figured one of you or both would get a little seasick. Most do the first time. He'll get over it."

"So is there anything I can do now?" I asked.

"We're having bacon and eggs and hash brown potatoes for breakfast," Alan said. "You can clean up about ten pounds of potatoes and get them boiled. Then we're done for now. Be here at about 600 hours."

"Six hundred, is that six o'clock?"

"Right, 6 AM... when it gets to 12 AM the next hour is 1300, we use a 24 hour clock."

"Okay got it. I'll go and see if Mark is still alive."

Chapter 14

Mark made it. He was a little queasy for the next day but soon he got his "sea legs" and felt fine. We did our job in the galley and the next day went past pretty uneventfully. The captain called down to the galley and asked if we were needed for an hour or so and Alan told him he was fine without us for a while. Then the captain invited us up to the wheelhouse to watch as we locked through the Soo Locks.

We went up to the wheelhouse one at a time so we wouldn't be noticed. Davey and John, the First Mate stood at the windows in front of the ship watching the lake ahead of us. John was at the big wheel used for steering.

"Ah, I thought you boys would like to see how we get this big girl from Lake Superior to the lower lakes," Captain McSorley said.

"Yes sir, that's very nice of you," I said.

"Davey, why don't you explain this to your bunkmates?"

Davey nodded. "I'd be glad to Captain. The Soo locks are the only way to get from Lake Superior to the other lakes. Lake Superior is 21 feet higher than the lower lakes. Before the locks were constructed the passage was made over the falls of the St. Mary's River. The locks bypass the rapids of the river and are at Sault St. Marie, Michigan. The first lock was constructed back in the late 1800's and others have been added over the years.

There are no pumps in the locks. Everything is done by gravity. When a ship is passing from the upper lake to the lower lakes, the lockmaster closes the doors on both ends of the lock. Then he fills the lock to the level of Lake Superior by opening valves that let water flow into the chamber using gravity to fill it. Then the upper door opens and the ship moves into the lock. They close the upper doors and then the lower valves are opened and again gravity releases the water and drops it to the level of the lower lake. Once the water levels are equal, the lower door opens and the ship moves out to the lower lake. Going up to Lake Superior the procedure is done the opposite way. It's very simple."

"That's quite amazing," I said. "How long does it take to lock through?"

"Usually about an hour" the Captain said.

"So do you want to stay up here and watch?" Davey asked.

"Alan said he didn't need us for an hour or two, that'd be great," Mark said.

John picked up the radio transmitter and talked to the lock and soon got the ok to proceed. He steered the ship for the lock and the big doors opened like they were in slow motion. Davey was standing at a second consol.

"Take her two degrees port," John said.

Davey touched a button and held it for about a minute.

"David is using the bow-thruster," the captain said. "There are thrusters in the bow that can help us turn to the port or starboard. Otherwise it's a chore to get something this long into a spot that small."

We watched spellbound as the bow nestled in between the walls of the lock. John made slight changes with the wheel and soon we were safely inside the huge chamber. John called to the engine room and told them to "All Stop".

The captain motioned to the back and we watched the big doors close. Then without any fanfare the water began to drop. The only way you could tell was that there was a wet line on the wall that was getting higher by the minute. In a few minutes the wet mark was 21 feet up on the wall.

The lockmaster blew one short toot on his horn and John answered with one short toot.

John called down to the engine room. "Ahead Slow," he said.

The lower doors were now open and we crept slowly out of the lock. "Take her 4 degrees to port," John said to Davey.

Soon the bow moved to the left a little and John told the engine room "All Ahead Full."

"Amazing," I said.

"It goes well when it's calm. We've hit the wall a few times but that's to be expected with something this big," Captain McSorley said.

"Thanks for letting us watch," I said.

"Yes thank you Captain," Mark added.

"We better get back and help Alan," I said moving to the door. Davey turned and nodded to us. He was plainly proud of his part helping lock through and glad we got to see him do it. I was getting to like the kid more and more.

We fed the crew lunch and then crossed Lake Huron uneventfully. Dinner came and went and later that evening we were in our room with Davey.

"That's pretty cool that they let you run that bow thruster," I said.

"Oh that's a no-brainer. They tell me how many degrees and I push a button. The real skill is at the wheel. That takes a lot of practice."

"The captain seems to be a really nice man," Mark said.

"He's the best. Actually all of the officers are real nice. I've never had any problems with any of them, or for that matter anyone on the ship. Usually there is a butthead or two but the *Fitzgerald* has a great crew of really nice guys. Captain McSorley has been the skipper for three years. He replaced Captain Peter Pulcer who had the nickname, the DJ Captain."

"The DJ Captain?" I asked.

"The *Fitzgerald* was a very popular ship for people to watch since it was so huge and so beautifully made. Captain Pulcer would blare loud music through the ships intercom system while they passed through the St. Claire and Detroit Rivers. People along the shore enjoyed his music and often when they'd lock through the Soo Locks he'd come out on deck with a bullhorn and tell the onlookers about the ship and the locks. He was quite a showman."

"He sounds like it," Mark said.

"I never met him but he also was well liked by all the crew. Captain McSorley isn't such a showman but he's a very good captain and well liked and respected by the whole ship."

"Well, he's sure been good to us," I said.

"He likes you guys and he's looking forward to some good pranks when we have some guests aboard. He's not above a good prank... that's for sure."

We had indeed been lucky when we ran into Thomas and Paul that day.

"Well, tomorrow we'll sail down the Detroit River and unload. We'll have about 14 hours with nothing to do," Davey said.

"We have to ask Thomas and Paul if they have a room here," Mark said. "If they do we can have a little party."

Chapter 15

A couple of meals later we were sailing down the Detroit River. It was quite a change from the open lake where all you could see was water to the Detroit River with a huge city and skyscrapers lining the shore. There was a lot of river traffic so they needed to be on their toes in the wheelhouse. Soon we turned into a huge dock and the deck hands scrambled to throw small ropes across to workers on the dock. The small ropes were attached to huge ropes used to tie the ship up and soon everything was made fast and the ship was docked.

The deck hands began to unfasten the hatch covers and cranes lifted them off. The elevators that would unload the taconite were lowered into the holds and unloading began.

We watched the whole operation with fascination and stayed out of the way with all the huge equipment that was being used. Soon Davey showed up.

"Have you talked to Thomas and Paul?" he asked.

"Yeah, they have a room here like they do in Duluth. They said they'd meet us here so we're waiting for them now. They said to invite you along too. Is it okay for you to leave the ship?"

"I have nothing to do really. I asked the captain and he said go have fun."

"Well an order is an order," Mark said grinning.

It wasn't long and Thomas and Paul showed up and we all left the ship. Their room was only six blocks from the waterfront so we walked down the streets toward it.

"We have to be back at the ship first thing in the morning," Davey said. "The captain said we plan to leave the dock at 700 hours."

"Then we can have a fine time in Detroit tonight," Paul said nodding.

"I think first we'll stop at the room and see if anyone else is there. Then we can go and get some pizzas and some beers and spend a little down time. Then a nap and maybe tonight we can check out the night life."

"You forget not all of us are 21," I said.

"Not to worry, we know the places that aren't too strict on that."

The room in Detroit was pretty much a dump as the one in Duluth.

"Enter," Paul said standing aside so we could walk into the ground floor hovel.

"This is as nice as the other one," I said.

Thomas and Paul laughed. "If you knew how little we pay for it you'd understand why it's so... Spartan."

"Well, it's got beds, a stove, a refrigerator and a toilet and shower. All the basics."

We tossed our duffle bags onto the floor and locked up and walked down the street to a pizzeria. It smelled wonderful inside and we took a large table and ordered some pizzas and two pitchers of beer. No IDs were asked for. We had the two pitchers gone before the pizza arrived and ordered two more when they delivered the pizzas. By the time we finished eating Davey was getting a little goofy.

"Dang, I'm glad we got some more younger guys on the ship," he giggled. "Now I got somebody to hang with."

We paid up and stopped at a beer store on the way back and got three 12 packs of beer to keep us hydrated for the rest of the afternoon. When we got back to the room we played penny anti poker and drank beer. Davey pooped out at about 4 in the afternoon and took a nap. The rest of us played on until the beer ran out. Then we all settled down for a nap of our own.

It was dark when Davey shook me.

"I thought we were going out," he said.

"I guess we all fell asleep," I said. I began waking everyone up and soon we were all heading for the bathroom and washing up. We headed down the street to a bar the guys knew of where they served good bar food and weren't too worried about the

61

age of the patrons.

The place was full of sailors and dockworkers and it was rocking. The music was loud and the place full of smoke and the smell of spilled beer. We found a booth in the corner and Thomas went up and ordered a pitcher of beer and 5 glasses. He asked for a waitress to take a food order too.

We were starting our first beers when a cute gal came up for our food orders. Each of us ordered a burger and fries. Then we ordered a large order of onion rings to snack on while we waited for the burgers. As she walked away Davey looked after her like he'd just fallen in love.

"Like that Davey?" Thomas asked.

"I like," he said grinning.

The evening passed and we drank several more pitchers of beer after we finished our burgers. Davey was getting pretty silly and we were having a lot of fun with him. It was pretty obvious he'd not done a lot of drinking before this night.

"There's that waitress again," he said looking across the floor.

"She's too much woman for you little man," Paul said.

"Baloney... I think she likes me, she winked at me a while ago."

We all laughed. "She probably had something in her eye Davey," Mark said.

"I'll prove it to you," he said and got to his feet. He walked a little unsteadily across the floor and stepped right up to the waitress. She was talking to a big curly haired guy with muscles on his muscles.

"Oh man," Thomas said.

Davey put his arm around the girl and kissed her on the neck. Then he turned and grinned at us.

The guy who the girl was talking to stood up and hit Davey in the side of the head with a punch we could hear all the way across the floor. Davey went down like a sack of sand.

"Oh no... well?" Paul said looking at the rest of us.

"He's our friend," Thomas said and nodded.

They got up and I looked at Mark. He shrugged so we got up and followed.

"Excuse me," Thomas said to the guy who'd hit Davey.

The guy turned and Thomas hit him right in the nose and he tipped over backwards.

From there on everything got very noisy and confused.

Guys from the bar jumped on each of us and soon there were fights going on all over the room. We each had a guy or two hitting us and taking hits from us, and then guys that had been in the bar before we got there began fighting each other.

It seemed to take quite a long time but it was probably only a few minutes until the lights came up and several policemen waded into the melee and began pulling people apart and handcuffing them. As I was being handcuffed I saw Davey sitting on the floor shaking his head looking confused. He looked up at me and grinned.

It was after midnight by the time we all were booked into the local precinct and put in the "drunk tank". The five of us were sitting together nursing bruised knuckles and a couple of black eyes.

Davey had a silly grin on his face. "Boy, that was something wasn't it?" he said.

We had to laugh but it hurt to do so.

Chapter 16

It hurt like heck to open my eyes. I looked around the cell to make sure I hadn't been dreaming when we were thrown into jail after the brawl in the bar downtown. Thomas was laying on the floor snoring, Paul lay beside him also sleeping and Mark was sitting up with his head against the block wall also sleeping. I looked to my left and Davey was sitting next to me rubbing his face. He only had one shoe on his right foot.

"How are you feeling?" I asked quietly.

He turned to me. "I hurt kinda bad but I'm okay. How about you?"

"I'm okay. My left eye feels kind of bad."

Davey turned and looked. His face showed surprise.

"You got a shiner like really bad," he said. "It's a dandy."

I had to laugh despite the fact it hurt like mad.

We looked around the room. We were in a basement and there were two cells. Both consisted of two outside walls of cement blocks and two inside walls of steel bars. There were three other guys in our cell. Two looked like sailors and the other was an old guy who looked like he was homeless.

Across the room the other cell held some of the guys who we'd been fighting with the previous night.

The old homeless guy stirred and farted.

Davey looked at me and grinned. "Nice one," he said.

Thomas stirred and slowly sat up. His hair was sticking out all over the place and he had a bruise on his cheek.

"What time is it?" he asked.

"I have no idea, they took everything from us," I said.

Just then the smell from the old guy's fart reached us.

"Holy crap... who did that?" Thomas said loudly.

Paul and Mark woke up and smelled the air.

"Thomas, you pig!" Paul said.

"It wasn't me, it was that old guy," Thomas said pointing to the man and pulling his tee shirt up over his nose.

Paul looked the best of all of us. He had a couple of scrapes on his chin but not much else. Mark looked pretty frazzled and had a cut lip that had swelled up pretty badly.

"Well, that was fun," Mark said stretching.

"We got to find out what time it is and let the captain know where we are. We're suppose to leave port at 700 hours," Davey said urgently.

Just then a door opened to the room and a jailer walked in and up to our cell.

"Are you the guys from the *Fitzgerald*?"

"Yes sir," Davey said.

The man opened the door. "Out! You've been bailed out."

We all staggered to our feet. The old homeless guy woke up and as we walked past him he joined us and started out of the door with us.

"Hold it a minute, where are you going?" the jailer asked him.

"I'm with these mates of mine," he said winking at us.

"Nice try," the jailer said and pushed him back into the cell.

"Tell the captain I'll be along directly," the old guy said to us.

We assured him we would tell him as soon as we saw him. We walked up the stairs and there was the First Mate standing in front of the desk talking to the sergeant in charge.

"Here are your men," the jailer said.

The First Mate stood there looking us up and down. He had a scowl on his face but we could tell he was trying hard to suppress a grin.

"You guys are lucky the sergeant here called the captain. Otherwise you'd be spending a week here with the fine officers of Detroit. The captain has bailed you out so you're free to come back to the ship. And just so you know, the bail money is coming out of your paychecks."

There was a chorus of "Aye Sir's."

There was a van waiting outside the precinct for us and we all piled in. The van headed to the waterfront and we all kept pretty quiet on the way.

"Whew," the First Mate said. "It smells like a stale brewery in here. When we get to the ship you guys get a shower and some breakfast and then report to the wheelhouse."

We all said, "Aye Sir."

It took about a half hour for all of us to shower and clean up. Then we reported to the galley. Alan had a huge grin on his face.

"Well, how nice of you to grace us with your presence," he said. "Does anyone require soft food?"

We all shook our heads no.

"Oh so no one lost any teeth? Ok, Mike and Mark, since you were detained I had a couple of the deck hands come down early this morning to take your place. So after your trip to the wheelhouse, I believe you guys will be doing the jobs those boys were scheduled to do today."

"That'll be fine Alan," I said.

He smiled. "Okay sit down and I'll fix you some breakfast. The coffee is fresh, get to it."

Soon two of the guys we knew from the deck carried in bowls of scrambled eggs and a plate of bacon and toast. When they saw Mark and me sitting next to each other they grinned.

"I TOLD you there was something fishy about that guy being so fast," one said.

Well, that was the end of our fooling the crew.

We reported to the wheelhouse and Captain McSorley was standing with his back to us as the ropes securing us to the dock were pulled in and put away. John was at the wheel and the Second Mate was at the bow thruster. We stood toward the back of the wheelhouse and waited.

"Okay John, take her out," the captain said.

John gave the engine room an "All Ahead Slow" and we began moving. "Four degrees port," he said to James the Second Mate. The ship slowly turned out into the Detroit River.

When we were well out in the river and picking up speed the captain turned to us.

66

"So," he said.

None of us said anything.

"When one person is late on a ship that person interferes with every other person on that ship. You five have wasted the time of 25 other men. Instead of being underway hours ago everyone has been sitting and waiting for you to return from your drunken brawl on shore."

"Captain, I want to say this was all my fault," Davey said.

"Is that right?"

"Yes sir. I had a tiny bit too much to drink and was a little to familiar with a young lady and her boyfriend took offense to it."

"You do understand that you above all of these men should know how important it is to be on time,"

"Yes Sir, I'm terribly sorry. It was not my intention to delay our departure. My inhibitions seem to have been soluble in alcohol and my better judgment got me in trouble but thanks to my shipmates here I came out of it well."

Captain McSorley stood there pursing his lips trying to keep from laughing. Finally he smiled and shook his head.

"And when your shipmates came to your defense the whole place went up like a prize fight?"

"That would be correct Sir."

"Well David, I'm proud of you for stepping up and taking the blame. I'm also proud of your mates for standing up for you. I guarantee this is not the first time this has happened. In fact I can remember a very similar situation when I was around your age. You all look like you came through it fairly well. How does the other side look?"

We all had to grin. "I think we made a good showing Sir," Thomas said.

"Well done."

"Sir we're very sorry we delayed the departure of the ship."

"We'll catch up... not to worry. But if I don't punish you the rest of the crew might feel like I'm playing favorites, so you four will take the job of swabbing the deck and let the normal deck hands have some down time for what they did to cover for your jobs. David, we'll find a task more fitting to an officer for you."

We all said thank you in unison.

"And next time, you guys keep your cadet under your care so we don't have a repeat incident. This was a mistake. A second time will be looked at as insubordination and I will not be able to overlook it."

We filed out of the wheelhouse feeling pretty lucky. Davey stopped us and had a tear in his eye.

"You know, I've always kind of been an outcast. Last year being a Maritime Cadet the crew on the ship I was on stayed away from me like I wasn't part of the crew. Then when I came to the *Fitzgerald*, Thomas and Paul were real decent to me. Now I feel like the five of us are true friends. That makes me really happy and I want to thank you guys for coming to my rescue and sticking up for me."

We all gave him a hug.

"Davey, you're one of the gang. We just have to get you a little more practice drinking beer so you won't get nuts on us again."

"I like to practice," he said beaming.

Chapter 17

The four of us reported to the Third Mate who was in charge of the deck hands. He showed us to a service room that was where the mops and cleaning equipment was stored.

"The seagulls leave their mark on the ship especially when we're in port, so when we set out on a voyage, the deck hands clean the deck and the hatch covers." He showed us buckets, mops and bottled soap. "There are 21 hatch covers and each is 11 feet wide by 48 feet long. Two start on one end of the ship and the other two at the other end and start swabbing the hatch covers with the mops. When you get one mopped, rinse it off with the big fire hoses. Then move on. The team that works hardest gets the honor of cleaning the extra hatch. Then when they're all clean, swab the deck between them and rinse everything into the lake. Any questions?"

We all shook our heads no.

"Okay, get at it boys," he said.

We decided to split up, one twin with Thomas and one with Paul. I ended up with Thomas and we filled our bucket with water and grabbed two mops and a bottle of soap and walked aft to the last cover to start cleaning. Mark and Paul stayed forward.

We took off our shoes and socks and rolled up our pants so we'd stay dry. Thomas gave the first cover a rinse with the hose to wet down the gull poop and then we climbed up on it and began swabbing it off.

"This isn't too bad," he said. "It's kind of nice to be out in the sunshine instead of down in the engine room."

"It's okay," I said. "I don't mind the galley, Alan is real decent to us and I kind of like to cook, but this is nice too."

We finished swabbing the cover and rinsed it and then moved to the next one. The sun was high in the sky so we took off our shirts and so did the other two at the other end of the boat. A little while later someone in the wheelhouse began playing Beach Boys music over the loudspeakers. That really got us grinning and what was suppose to be a punishment turned out to be a pretty fine day.

We cleaned all day, stopping only for a lunch brought up to us by Davey. Alan packed a cooler with sandwiches and some fruit for us.

"So what are you doing?" I asked Davey.

"I'm polishing all of the brass fittings in the wheelhouse. I had no idea how much brass there was. I'll probably still be at it when we get back to Duluth."

"Well, it could be worse," Mark said.

"Yeah, I think we all got off easy. We'll have to be more careful next time on shore."

"What do you mean WE?"

Davey grinned, "Well, me I guess."

Working on deck we saw other ships passing either going "upbound" or "downbound". "Upbound" meant a ship was traveling up the lake to the highest lake, Superior, while "downbound" meant they were traveling from Superior to one of the lower lakes. Often all we'd see was the smoke from the engines on the horizon. Sometimes we passed within a mile or so of the other ships.

"It's amazing how much water there is here," I said to Thomas.

"The Great Lakes are the largest group of freshwater lakes on earth. They contain 21% of all the fresh water in the world and cover over 94 thousand square miles. I read that about a billion years ago two tectonic plates split apart and created the Mid-continent Rift which created a valley that formed a basin that formed Lake Superior. Then the St. Lawrence Rift formed about half a billion years ago and created Lake Huron, Michigan and Erie.

"When the last glaciers melted about 10,000 years ago the melt water filled up these basins and the Great Lakes were formed. I've been diving and it's amazing down there. You can see how the glaciers scoured the land and deposited piles of boulders and left behind hills and valleys. It's like looking back 10,000 years because erosion hasn't changed things like they've changed on land."

"You've been diving in Lake Superior?"

"Yeah, I worked one summer for the DNR on some lake trout projects. If we ever get a few extra days off I have a friend who still dives a lot. I bet he'd take us out on a dive if you'd like to try it."

"I've never done it. Do you think someone with zero experience should be diving on Lake Superior?"

"Well, we'd start in close to shore and work our way out."

"Sounds good," I said.

"There are hundreds of shipwrecks on the bottom of not only Superior but the other lakes too. Many have been found and you can get the coordinates and go and explore them. There are wrecks as far back as the 1600s"

"Wow, that's cool. They're still intact?"

"The bottom is very cold. Lake Superior is about 34 degrees at the bottom. It's also very low oxygen so anything that ends up down there is pretty much preserved by the cold and lack of oxygen. Some of the wrecks look like they went down yesterday and they really sank a hundred years ago."

"Amazing, I hope we can do that this summer," I said.

"We'll get you out on Gitche Gumee and let you see it all," he said.

"Gitche Gumee, is that Superior?"

"That's what the Chippewa called it... it means Big Lake."

I nodded. "Well they got that right for sure."

I felt cold water on my back and turned just in time to see the stream of water from Mark and Paul's hose coming across the last hatch cover that was between us. Thomas picked up our hose and turned it on them and in no time the four of us were soaked to the skin.

We finally called a truce and all gathered on the last cover and began working on it together. We all were a little sunburned but happy after a day in the sunshine and feeling much better after our early morning hangover.

We finished the last cover and then went back to each end and began cleaning the deck and rinsing everything into the lake. Half an hour later we were approaching the middle of the ship again, almost finished.

Thomas nudged me. "Look here comes Davey," he said quietly.

"I'll alert Mark," I said.

"Mark, Davey is coming down the deck and he looks pretty thirsty."

Mark looked over at me and grinned and said something to Paul.

We all looked away like we hadn't seen Davey coming and when he got even with us on the deck we turned both hoses on him. The look on his face was priceless and it was even funnier when his hat flew off and over the side pushed by a stream of water.

"You... you!" Davey stood there dripping with an amazed look on his face.

"We're even," Thomas said.

Davey grinned. "Okay, I guess I had that coming. But you guys better sleep with one eye open from now on."

Chapter 18

We all slept really soundly that night. In fact the alarm clock took a long time to wake us at 5 AM the next morning.

"Jeez, get out of here and let me sleep," Davey growled.

"My my... touchy," Mark said. We dressed and washed up and when we got ready to leave I slapped Davey on the ass.

"See you at breakfast Sunshine."

Alan had a smirk on his face when we walked into the galley. He gave us each a job to do and we got to the task of preparing 30 breakfasts.

When the crew began arriving to eat we got a lot of crap from them not only about getting tossed into the Drunk Tank, but about getting busted with our twin act.

"We won't know you apart once your faces heal but at least we'll know there are two of you turds," one of the deck hands said with a grin.

After breakfast Mark and I cleaned up the galley while Alan took some time off to rest. When we were finished we walked up on deck and sat on a bench to watch the ship lock through the Soo Locks again. It was an amazing thing to see a ship that was as long as two football fields slide into a lock that was just barely wide enough for it to fit.

"I wouldn't want to drive the boat when they lock through," Mark said.

"Me either, and I think it's a ship," I said.

Once we locked through we got up to speed and started up across Lake Superior. We went to the galley and helped with lunch and dinner and then went to bed again, still a little tired out from our night on the town in Detroit.

The next morning after breakfast Davey came into the galley and told us we should be in the harbor in a couple of hours.

"We'll tie up and then have a couple of days off," he said. "We have to take on fuel and then we'll load up with Taconite again and off we go to Detroit."

"How much gas does it take to fill this thing?" Mark asked.

"It takes 72,000 gallons of fuel oil," Davey replied.

"Holy cow, I'd hate to pay the bill for that," I said.

"So what will you do while we're onshore?" Mark asked Davey.

"Oh I usually just stay on the ship and read or rest," he said.

"You know, Thomas and Paul have a room rented and we're staying with them. I'm sure you'd be welcome to come and spend a couple of days with us there. They've got four beds but a whole closet full of air mattresses and blankets. It'd be a lot better than sitting here alone."

Davey brightened up. "Do you think they'd mind?"

"I don't think they'd mind a bit, in fact I'm sure they'd be happy to have you along. We're buddies, we went to prison together."

Davey laughed. "Please, don't remind me."

"I'll talk to Paul and Thomas and let you know."

Later I went down to the engine room. It was loud as heck. I walked around for a bit looking and then saw Thomas tinkering with a dial on one of the big machines. He was wearing earmuffs to deaden the sound. He saw me and motioned up some stairs and I followed him to the deck.

"What's up?" he asked.

"We're going to be in Duluth for a couple of hours. Do you think it'd be ok to ask Davey to come with us?"

He grinned. "That'd be fine. He's a pretty good kid. He's got balls too. I don't think I'd have had the guts to go up to that girl in the bar like he did. Sure, ask him to come. We'll have fun."

Several hours later, the *Fitzgerald* was safely tied to the dock. Most of the crew was headed out for shore leave and the five of us were right among them. Captain McSorley stood on the deck of the wheelhouse and looked down at us and smiled.

"Have a good time boys... and stay out of jail," he said.

We assured him we would be very careful about going to jail again.

Tigger was very glad to see us. No one was at the room and it looked like the last person had filled her food and water bowls for her some time ago because both were nearly empty. She rubbed up against us and checked out Davey. It didn't take long and she was cozying up to him too.

"I never really liked cats," he said, "but she's pretty sweet."

There was a knock on the door at the top of the stairs and I walked down the hall and opened it. Henry was standing there smiling.

"I saw you guys drive up," he said.

"Come on in Henry, it's good to see you," I said opening the door.

Everyone was glad to see Henry and we introduced him to Davey.

"So how was your voyage?" he asked.

"The voyage was fine, but we got thrown into jail in Detroit," Paul said.

Henry smiled. "Do tell."

We explained the circumstances to him and he grinned at Davey.

"It's always the small one who starts it," he said grinning.

Davey just blushed.

"So did you guys know the smelt are running?" Henry asked.

"That what?" I asked.

"Smelt... they're a small fish the size of a big minnow. They're in the lake by the millions and at this time of year they "run" close to shore. They're spawning now and they come into shallow water to lay their eggs and the males fertilize them. They're good eating. You can dip them by the thousand."

"Wow that sounds like fun," Mark said. "But we don't have any equipment."

"I have a seine net and several pairs of chest waders. My sons used to dip smelt when they were young and I ended up with all the equipment."

"It sounds like fun, let's go," Thomas said.

"Oh you can't do it during the day. They're sensitive to sunlight and they stay in deep water during the day, but they run at night. But we can get all the stuff ready and go out tonight if you guys have nothing else planned."

"We promised the captain we'd stay out of jail," I said.

Henry laughed. "Then this will be just the activity for a good night of fun."

Chapter 19

We had some time to kill since it was several hours until it would be dark, so Thomas and Mark drove to the market and got some food so we could eat before we set out with Henry to fish for smelt.

"So these smelt... they're just minnows?" I asked.

"Well," Henry said, "they aren't a native species in the Great Lakes.   Back in 1912 they escaped from an inland lake in Michigan where they had been stocked as a forage fish for walleyes and bass. Once they got into Lake Michigan it didn't take long until they began to show up in Lake Superior and the rest of the Great Lakes. For a long time they stayed in pretty manageable numbers until the sea lamprey arrived."

"Where did the lampreys come from" Paul asked.

"When the St. Lawrence Seaway was opened it allowed ships to come into the Great Lakes from the ocean. When you open a waterway like that, other things use it too and the sea lamprey found their way into the lakes. They were happy when they found one of the native species in the lakes was lake trout and their numbers exploded as they preyed on the lake trout."

"They killed them?"

"Well eventually most of the trout that got attacked died. The lamprey attaches with a sucker mouth full of teeth and chews a hole into the side of the trout. Lake trout have a soft skin and small scales that are easy to chew through. When the lamprey was full, he'd drop off. Usually another hooked onto the same trout or there were already others attached. Some trout had a dozen lampreys hanging on them. Eventually many of the trout died out and that left a hole in the predator/prey situation. The trout had been feeding heavily on smelt. When the numbers of trout declined the numbers of smelt increased. Soon the spawning runs of them turned into millions of fish and someone figured out that they were good eating. So it didn't take long and people started finding ways of catching them."

"What should we expect?" Davey asked.

"Well there are several ways of doing it. One way is to just wade out with a big dip net with fine mesh. Then you dip it into the water and come up with some smelt. You might get 6 or 60 or 600 depending on your timing and luck. Another way is with a pull seine and you get one guy on each end and pull it along the beach and trap a bunch of smelt in the seine. Then you pull them up in shallow water and dip them out of the seine into buckets. My sons and I used to just go down to Park Point here in Duluth and net them. All we need is a fishing license and we're set. I have all of the rest of the gear."

"It sounds like fun," I said, "so are they good to eat?"

"They're great eating," Henry said. "Some people just dip them in beer batter head, guts and all and deep fry them. I prefer taking the heads off and slitting the belly to pull the guts out. Then all we need is a big pot of hot oil, some fried potatoes, some baked beans and something to wash them down, and we'll have a feast you'll never forget."

I looked at Davey and he was grinning. "That sounds great, especially that part about the beverages to wash it down."

"Davey, I do think you're becoming an alcoholic," I said laughing.

"Well, we have to buy some beer to make the beer batter, we don't want the extra to go to waste do we?"

I had to agree with his logic.

Thomas and Mark came back with a bunch of hot dogs and buns and some salads from the deli at the market. There was a little camp charcoal grill under the kitchen sink so we set it out on the landing at the top of the steps and fired it up. In no time we had a pile of grilled weenies and several salads to choose from. As we ate we told Thomas and Mark about the smelt fishing and they were looking forward to it as much as we were.

We napped and played cards and just wasted the rest of the

afternoon. About an hour before dark we drove to Henry's house. He lived just a block from the lake in a small bungalow with a small garage next to it. He went inside the garage and opened the big door. Inside were many fishing poles and other gear including four pairs of chest waders and a seine that was rolled up with about a six-foot pole attached to each end.

"The waders are different sizes but they were all for boys your age so try them on to see who fits what."

It turned out that Thomas was without waders. His size thirteen feet didn't come close to the sizes available. There were two waders in size 10, which fit Mark and me perfectly. One pair was size 11 which fit Paul and the other was a size 9, which fit Davey with a little tugging.

Thomas brought the net and we carried four plastic buckets out of the garage. Henry had two small dip nets with fine mesh in his hand.

"We can just walk down to the point from here," Henry said.

We followed Henry down the street to the lake. The street ended in a dead end with a barricade to stop someone from driving into the lake. We crossed the beach and stopped at the water's edge. There were several other groups of smelt fishermen scattered up and down the beach.

"Okay, let's get the seine rolled out and ready. Once it gets dark we'll start," Henry said.

While we rolled out the net, Davey and Mark carried a couple of armloads of driftwood down by us and piled it up to make a bonfire. There were many more fires up and down the beach. Henry took a little can of lighter fluid from his pocket and squirted some on the wood and touched a match to it.

"I learned that in Boy Scouts," he said winking his eye.

We were all anxious to get started but none of the other fishermen had waded out yet so we also waited.

"This is going to be really cool," Davey said to me with his eyes flashing from the flickering fire. "I've never done anything outdoorsy like this."

"Well, I've done some outdoors stuff but never anything quite like this," I said.

Soon we saw other groups wading out and looked at Henry for the go-ahead.

"Well, two of you take the seine, the other two stay next to the beach with the dip nets and Thomas you ready the buckets."

We all nodded and Mark took one end of the seine while Davey grabbed the other pole.

"Okay, wade out carefully and one of you stay closer to the beach while the other swings out. Then the one out in deeper water should swing around toward the beach and make a trap for the smelt inside the net. If we're lucky there will be a bunch. Then the two with the little nets need to get in there and dip them out of the purse in the net and dump them into buckets. You have to move quickly or they'll swim out of the trap."

Mark and Davey started out into the ice-cold water of Lake Superior and we stood waiting for the smelt to arrive.

Chapter 20

"Be careful how far you go out, it drops off pretty fast," Henry warned.

The two net draggers replied that they'd be careful. Mark stayed closer to land and Davey waded out until he was about waist deep. Then they started pulling the net through the water parallel to shore. They went about thirty feet when Henry told Davey to wade toward the shore. Davey pulled the net in towards shore and Thomas and Paul and I met them on the beach. They pulled the net up close to the beach and we could see several small silver fish flopping in the net.

"You guys dip them out with the small nets and put them into the pail," Henry directed.

Paul and I caught the little fish and took them to Thomas who was holding the pail. We dumped them into the pail. Thomas looked down and counted.

"We got eleven," he said.

"Well that's not very good," Henry said. "At this rate we'll be here for a week to get enough for a smelt fry. Try another pull," he said to Mark and Davey.

They walked back into the water and started pulling the net again. This time they went a little farther and when they pulled it up to the beach there were a lot more smelt in the net. We dipped them out and there were enough to fill half of the bucket.

"They're starting to move," Henry said. "Try another pull."

The next pull yielded over a pail of the small silver fish. We were getting pretty excited when we saw so many in the net. We dipped them all out and Mark and Davey went right back in for another pull. This time we got another pail and then some.

"We've probably got more than we need," Henry said.

"One more pull," Davey said. "We're just getting good at this."

The two seine pullers waded back into the lake.

"Let's go a little deeper," Davey said.

Mark moved out about ten feet to deeper water and Davey moved out the same distance. They turned and began a pull. I heard a little yelp and Davey disappeared. One second he was there and the next second he was gone.

Suddenly he surfaced like one of those big blue whales when they come up from the bottom of the ocean.

"Holy crap!" he screamed.

He stumbled around and went under again but came right back up. Mark began pulling the net toward him.

"Grab the net I'll pull you in," he yelled to Davey.

Paul and I waded in toward Davey to help him. He was stumbling around and trying to get to his feet. His waders were full of ice-cold lake water and he must have weighed seventy pounds more than usual from all the water in the waders.

We finally got hold of him and dragged him up onto the sand.

"Oh man, cold," he said through shivering teeth.

Henry was laughing so hard he had to sit down on one of the buckets.

"I knew it would happen," he said bent over with laughter.

Davey was lying on his back on the beach. I took one of his feet and Paul took the other and we lifted them up and water began to flow out of the top of his waders onto the sand. When many gallons of water had drained from the boots we dropped his feet and each of us took one of his hands and pulled him up.

"Frozen," he chattered.

"Get his waders off and get him next to the fire," Henry said still laughing.

We helped Davey strip off the waders and then helped him next to the fire. Steam was coming off his clothes.

"Get those wet clothes off," Thomas said.

"What here? There are other people here," Davey said.

"Well do you want to warm up or stand there and freeze?"

He wasn't happy about it but he took off his shirt and tee shirt. His hands were so cold he couldn't unbutton his jeans so

Paul helped him. Then Paul and I pulled his jeans and socks off.

"That's far enough," he said. "I'm not going to stand here with my wiener hanging out."

"As cold as that water is, someone would need a magnifying glass to see it," Thomas said.

We all laughed and even Davey had to laugh.

"If I had to pee right now, I'd have to sit down."

Davey got warmed up and Thomas gave him his flannel shirt. It was big enough that it fit Davey like a nightshirt. We gathered up the gear and Davey's clothes and hiked back up the beach.

When we got to Henry's house we put away the gear and hung Davey's waders upside down so they could dry out. Henry set up a folding table and we sat on stools to begin cleaning the smelt.

"You know what would make this go a lot faster?" Thomas said.

"Barley Pop?"

Thomas nodded. "I'll run down the block. I saw a tavern there. You guys start and I'll get some refreshment."

Henry brought out some tools. He had a garden pruning shears, two small paring knives and two toothbrushes.

"Okay, one guy nip the heads off, then toss them over to the two with the knives. Those two cut open the belly and the two with the toothbrushes scrape out the guts. Then put the clean fish in a bucket."

We all understood the jobs and sat down to start on four 5gallon buckets of smelt.

Thomas got back with a 24 pack of beer and when he took over the pruning shear job Henry just sat and watched and drank beer. When the bucket of clean fish got about three quarters full he took it and rinsed the fish off with a water hose.

We sat and talked and laughed and had a grand time. The time went past very quickly and it didn't seem to take very long and all of the fish were cleaned.

"What time is it?" Mark asked.

"It's almost 2:30 am," Henry said looking at his watch.

"Holy smokes that time went fast," I said. "I was hoping to have a fish fry yet."

"I'll put the fish in some coolers with ice and we'll have our fish fry tomorrow," Henry said. "Right now this old man is due for bed."

We all realized we were getting pretty tired too, so we bid Henry a good night and walked up the street. We were tired. Davey was wearing nothing but a shirt and damp underwear, and we all smelled like fish, but we'd had a great night and one that we'd not soon forget.

When we got to Chez-Dump we washed up and were in bed with in a few minutes.

"What a good time."

"No kidding. We're going to have to remember that and come back up here again and do that next year."

Little did I know then that another smelt fishing trip was not going to ever happen for Mark and me.

Chapter 21

The next morning none of us was up very early. I heard Thomas blast a couple of times and opened my eyes and looked around the room. Tigger was snuggled up against Davey's chest and he had his arm around her. He looked like he was about 12 years old with his kitty sleeping in his arms.

Thomas blasted again and then everyone began to stir. Paul sat up on the edge of his bed and sniffed the air.

"Whew, something's dead in here," he said.

Thomas began laughing and blasted again. I got up and opened the windows. There was a nice breeze blowing in off the harbor, which helped clear the air.

Over the next minutes everyone got up and took their turns in the bathroom. We had a light breakfast of cereal and toast since we were planning on gorging on smelt later and we all wanted to be really hungry for the feast.

Henry had given us a grocery list before we left the night before and suggested we take a couple of the pails of smelt to the *Fitzgerald* and have a smelt feed on the ship. What we didn't eat today at our feed would be frozen in Henry's freezer for another feast some day in the future.

Paul and I volunteered to go get the pails of smelt and take them to the ship and then get the groceries. The others were going to do the laundry we'd accumulated on the trip to Detroit.

Henry met us at the door and we got the two pails of smelt. He had a big pot hanging from a tripod over a propane heater already set up in front of the garage. "I'll expect you guys about 4 o'clock?"

"I can hardly wait," I said. "I'm hungry already."

We loaded the smelt into the car and drove down to the dock where the ship was tied up. We could see Captain McSorley up in the wheelhouse. Each of us took a pail and climbed the gangplank and when we got to the deck he'd come out of the wheelhouse and was standing at the railing of the walkway that surrounded it.

"So what are we smuggling aboard?" he said with a grin.

"Smelt Sir," I said, "we went smelting last night and got four 5 gallon pails of them. We're having a feed tonight and then we thought we could put these in the cooler and have a good feed when we get underway tomorrow."

The captain smiled. "That's very generous of you, and I'm sure that will be very appreciated by the crew. Did David participate?"

Paul began laughing. "He sure did Sir. He and I ran the seine and Davey ended up stepping off into some deep water and filled up his waders. We had to drag him ashore and strip him so he could warm up by the bonfire. It was pretty funny."

Captain McSorley laughed. "David seems to be very happy now that he's made friends with you guys. I'm glad you include him. Sometimes sailors are a little funny about associating with officers, even if they are cadets."

'Davey's cool," I said. "We enjoy having him with us."

"Well, I'm sure you can get those fish stowed away without help, so we'll see you tomorrow at about 1500 hours."

"Aye Sir," we said.

We went down to the galley and put the pails of fish into the walk-in cooler. Then we left a note for Alan to let him know where they'd come from. We went back topside and climbed down to the car and drove off the dock.

Paul knew of a good market and we stopped and picked up potatoes, coleslaw and of course some beer. We stopped at the Laundromat and found the other guys just finishing up with the clothes. With the clothes and groceries in the trunk we were pretty well packed on the trip back to the room.

We ate a few cookies and had a soda for lunch. We didn't want to eat a lot so we could fill up on smelt later. Then we got a game of poker going and passed the afternoon playing cards. Tigger sat on Davey's lap the whole time.

"I think she likes you," I said.

"It's probably because I smell like the lake," he said grinning.

"The captain said to be back by 1500 hours tomorrow," I told the group.

"We're going to Cleveland this time," Davey said.

"That takes about two days longer," Thomas added.

"So if no one is here when we leave, we better give Tigger an extra big dish of food and water," Mark said as he reached over and petted the cat.

About 3:30 we packed up the groceries and beer and drove over to Henry's place. He was in the driveway sitting in a lawn chair when we arrived. He'd set up a folding table next to the cooking pot and had a bunch of bowls and utensils piled on it.

"Ah, the hungry sailors arrive," he said getting up from his chair.

"Starved sailors," I said.

"Well, then let's get started," he said. He turned on the propane under the pot of oil and lit a flame to it. Soon the heater was warming the oil and we were gathered around waiting for some food.

"First go inside and wash the potatoes," Henry said. "Then two of you can cut them into French fries and the other two can help me batter and fry the fish. Put the rest of the food, on the table and the beer into that cooler," he directed.

Twenty minutes later the big pot of oil was ready. Henry put a thermometer into it and it was just at 375 degrees. He opened a covered bowl that contained his famous beer batter. Then he took a handful of smelt and dropped them into the batter and swished them around, coating them. He took those fish out and dropped them into the oil and added a second handful to them a minute later. The oil foamed up and the fish began to sizzle.

"Oh man," Davey said looking down into the bubbling oil.

Henry stirred the fish with a long spoon to get them apart from each other. Then when they were golden brown he began fishing them out of the oil with a long handled sieve. He had a cake pan lined with paper towels waiting and dumped the fish into it. Then he salted them and offered us a taste. To say the fish were good would be like saying Lake Superior was pretty big. The fish were fantastic. We all grabbed paper plates and shoveled a few onto them and began eating them when they were still way too hot.

"Oh man," Thomas said chewing on one of the succulent little morsels.

"Put a couple of handfuls of fries into the oil next" Henry said.

I dropped the fries in and they boiled up like the fish had earlier. In about 5 minutes they were golden brown and Henry fished them out and dumped them into the now empty fish pan.

He battered another batch of fish and into the oil they went.

Meanwhile we'd opened the rest of the food, the coleslaw and salads and began eating in earnest. Beers flowed, fish fried and we had an absolutely wonderful afternoon. It took about an hour of frying alternate batches of fish and fries to finally fill all of us up. It was probably one of the most memorable meals I'd ever eaten.

"Should I put some more in?" Henry asked.

"Not for me," I said.

There was a round of "Me either" so Henry shut off the propane. He had filled his plate many times during the feast too.

"Well," he said, "what do you think of smelt now?"

"I think I've been missing out for my whole life," Mark said.

"Who'd ever think that something I'd have thought of as bait would be so delicious?" Thomas said.

Henry just smiled and sat back in his chair.

Chapter 22

We said goodbye to Henry and promised to let him know when we got back into Duluth. Then we went back to the room and sat around talking until one by one we all got tired and went to bed.

The next morning no one was very hungry so we skipped breakfast. We got our gear ready to go back to the ship and after lunch we filled Tigger's bowls full of food and water and said goodbye to her.

When we arrived at the ship the loading was just finishing up. First Mate John waved to us from the wheelhouse. We all went to our quarters and dropped off our bags and then went to our posts. Mark and I went right to the galley after we'd changed into our cook's whites.

"It looks like we're having a smelt feed," Alan said grinning as we walked in.

"I hope it's okay with you," Mark said. "We got 4 pails of the things and thought it would be a nice meal for the crew."

"It's great," Alan said, "also, two big-wigs from the company are going with us to Cleveland, so this will impress the heck out of them."

We got busy and started preparing for the evening meal. Alan decided we should make hash brown potatoes so we could use both of our deep fryers for fish and keep them moving out fresh for the crew. While I was chopping cabbage for coleslaw I felt the hatch covers being lowered into place over the holds and soon I could feel the engines running, making a vibration in the deck.

Mark and Alan cooked a huge pot of potatoes and let them cool for hash browns and then Alan decided fresh baked dinner rolls would make a nice addition to the meal so they stirred up bread dough.

We were humming right along and the afternoon slipped

past very quickly. Davey showed up later and offered to help. Alan had him set up the two dining rooms and then they set up a buffet so we could put everything out and keep filling the serving container with fresh fish.

A while later Thomas and Paul showed up.

"The captain said we should come and help since we were in on the catching of the smelt," Paul said.

Alan got them a couple of Steward's jackets so they could act as waiters for the important table with the officers and the guests. Soon the crew began to arrive and they were really full of smiles when they saw the feast we'd prepared. There were compliments all around and they got right to it gobbling down smelt. Alan and I kept frying fish and Mark kept shuttling fresh fish to the buffet.

Soon the guests showed up with the captain and they were seated in the second dining room. The other officers were already eating. Alan had Mark and me fill some platters with fish and potatoes and the other stuff and serve the important guests rather than have them serve themselves like the rest of the crew. Mark took a platter of fish and potatoes in and set it in front of them. Then he came back and as he left the room I walked in with the rest of the food. The captain suppressed a smile as we passed each other. The two guests, older gentlemen looked up and then took a double take. They both looked curiously at me but said nothing. I put the food on the table and asked if there was anything else I could get them.

"Maybe a pot of coffee?" one asked.

I nodded yes and walked to the door. Mark was coming with the coffee so I let him enter and then walked out. I looked over my shoulder and Captain McSorley was nearly choking trying to keep a straight face.

A while later everyone was pretty much finished eating. The captain stuck his head into the galley and complimented us on the fine meal.

"Those guests are still scratching their heads over how fast you are," he said chuckling.

We had fried all but a small bowl of smelt. There was about enough for two people left when every one finally stopped eating. Thomas came into the galley and told us to come out to the dining room. Alan and I were covered with flour and beer batter and we all were pretty worn out keeping up feeding them. They all stood and gave us a hand.

It was a great start to a new voyage. Thomas and Paul stayed after everyone had left and helped us clean up. When everything was shining and clean we left Alan who was heading for his quarters and walked up on the deck.

We were out of sight of land and the moon was nearly full. You could see for miles and miles and all there was to see was flat calm water.

"You don't see Superior as flat as a millpond very often," Thomas said.

"It's really quite beautiful with the moon shining like it is," Davey replied. "I think this is why I want to make my living on the water. There're not a lot of people who see something like this."

Just then a meteorite streaked across the sky. We watched it until it blinked out.

"Very cool," Mark said.

"Well guys," I said, "this old sailor is ready for his rack."

There were nods all around. We filed down the hatchway and Thomas and Paul said goodnight and walked down the hall to their room.

We went into our quarters and undressed and got into our bunks. The curtain was pulled back from the porthole and we could see the moon shining through it.

"You know," Davey said, "I've always kind of been the odd duck. I mean when I was in school I was the kid who read books about the ocean and sailors. When everyone else was reading Sports Afield, I was reading Moby Dick or 20,000 Leagues under the Sea. When I went to the Maritime Academy I found that there were others like me who are drawn to the water. Now that I've met you guys and gotten to be friends with you and Thomas and Paul I know I made the right choice."

"So you plan to stick with it?" I asked.

"I know I'll stick with it. I'll live... and maybe die on the water."

Chapter 23

The next morning Mark and I were cleaning up after breakfast when Davey came hurrying into the galley.

"Hey, guess what," he said.

"I give up," I said.

"I'm going to steer through the Soo Lock today," he said excitedly.

"Holy cow, you're going to drive?" Mark asked.

Davey nodded up and down.

"The captain said it was time for me to make my first lock-through."

"Wow, that's pretty cool," I said. "I'll make sure to have my life vest on."

Davey gave me a dirty look.

"We'll be at the lock in about an hour. If you guys aren't busy come up and watch me... okay?"

"We'll be there," Mark said.

Davey hurried out and Mark turned to me.

"You think he's a little excited?"

"I just hope he doesn't hit something," I responded.

Forty-five minutes later we hiked up to the bow of the ship and sat on some benches below the wheelhouse. Davey was at the wheel and looked down at us and waved. First Mate John was at the bow thruster.

The lock was about a mile in the distance and soon we began to turn toward it. Davey blew the horn three times to signal the lockmaster that he wanted to lock through. A few seconds later there was one short toot that meant to come ahead. The end of the lock had two lights that looked like traffic signals. At the moment they showed red but soon turned yellow and the huge gates began to slowly open outward. Each of the gates was nearly forty feet long, made of steel and thick timbers. They took a long time to move through the water. We were about two hundred yards from the lock when the lights turned green.

The lockmaster gave one toot on his horn and Davey answered with a single toot. Looking at the opening and knowing it was just a few inches wider than the *Fitzgerald* made the procedure all the more exciting. We looked up at Davey in the wheelhouse and he was concentrating on getting the ship centered in the lock. We saw him say something to John at the bow thruster.

We were only a few yards from the lock entrance and everything looked pretty well lined up. I looked up and saw Davey look over to John and say something. John shook his head no. We moved forward a few more feet and the bow entered the lock.

Mark looked back toward the stern of the ship.

"It looks like we're going kind of crooked," he said.

Just then we felt a huge jolt and heard a dull "Boom" as the starboard side of the bow hit the lock wall. Davey looked like he was ready to jump overboard but Captain McSorley stood next to him and calmly gave him instructions. The bow scraped along the lock wall for about ten feet and by then we were lined up and it stopped scraping.

I looked up and Davey looked like he had crapped his pants. The captain was nodding and talking to him and seemed to be reassuring him. Davey glanced down at us and shook his head. We shrugged and grinned.

It took about twenty minutes for the entire ship to get into the lock. Then the big doors at the upper end closed. Meanwhile the deck hands tied some ropes to cleats on the lock wall. Without any fanfare the ship began to drop down along the wall of the lock. The water from the upper side left through huge tunnels under the lock walls and the chamber emptied silently and very swiftly. In no time we were twenty feet lower than we'd been at the beginning.

The lock doors on the lower side of the lock opened and the lockmaster gave a toot on his horn to proceed out. Davey answered with one toot and we began to move out into Lake Huron. Once we'd cleared the lock Mark and I walked over to the starboard side and looked at the side of the ship.

"Ouch," Mark said looking at the long scrape on the paint."

"Nothing a few quarts of paint won't fix," I said.

Just as we turned back from the side Davey walked up. His face was as red as if he'd been out in the sun way too long.

"Shit, my first time and I hit the damn lock!" he said shaking his head.

"Well, I'm sure that's not the first time," I said.

"Oh it's been done before but not by me. The captain probably will never let me drive again," he said.

He looked over the side and got a wounded look on his face.

"Yikes, that left a mark," he said grinning.

"Do they have any paint on board?" I asked.

"Yeah, I'm sure the deck boss has some, why?"

"How about we'll help you fix it?"

"I don't have to fix it, that's not my job."

"I know that but it'd look like a nice gesture if you fixed your screw-up."

"Yeah I guess you're right, I'll look into it."

"When you get the paint, get three brushes," Mark said.

Davey grinned. "Okay, and thanks."

Half an hour later Davey came back wearing some work clothes carrying some paint and brushes and two swing-like things.

"We have to hang these over the side and then climb down onto them to paint the scrape," he said.

"You mean we have to go over the side?"

Davey nodded. "Usually we do it in port but since it's so nice and calm the deck boss said it'd be okay now."

I looked at Mark.

"I'll go over the side with Davey," he said. "Mike's scared of heights. We'll leave him on top to hand us stuff."

That was just fine with me.

We hung the two swings over the side and checked that they were at the right height. Then we secured the ropes from them to a cleat on the deck. Mark and Davey took off their shirts and stepped up to the side of the ship. I pulled one of the swings up so it was just over the side and Davey climbed over and sat on the board. He fastened a harness that was attached to the rope around his chest and nodded to me.

"Let me down," he said.

I let the rope out until it stopped. Mark and I looked over the side. Davey was sitting there with his feet swinging back and forth about twenty feet above the lake.

"Nothin to it," he said grinning up at us.

Mark went over next and I could see a little fear as he slipped over the side onto the seat. He fastened his harness and down he went to the end of the rope. Then I tied the pail of paint onto a rope and tied the two brushes onto the rope and let it down to them. I looked over the side and they were sitting a few feet apart with a paintbrush in their hand painting the scrape.

I looked up to the wheelhouse; Captain McSorley was watching with a big smile. He nodded his approval.

A while later they'd painted the area where they were sitting. We had to move them a little aft to finish. Mark put his feet against the side of the ship and pushed away and I pulled on the rope moving it aft. He was in place to finish so I moved the pail of paint. Davey tied his paintbrush onto the rope and climbed up the rope to the top rail. I grabbed his hand and helped him over the side. We pulled his seat up and by the time we had it untied Mark was finished. We pulled up the paint and Mark climbed up and over the side and we were done.

I looked over the side and the ship looked like it was new.

"Not a bad job," I said.

Davey looked at the repair job too. "If this ship captain thing doesn't work out for me maybe I have a future in painting."

"Well I think that would be better than something like bus driver," I said.

Chapter 24

The rest of the voyage went without a hitch. We continued on to Cleveland and unloaded. The five of us managed to stay out of jail and we left the next morning for the harbor in Duluth. We crossed Lake Superior and as we came into Duluth harbor we were standing on deck with our duffle bags packed. Word had come that we'd be in port only two days while the ship was loaded with another load of taconite so we had little time to waste. We wanted to do our laundry have a few beers and then it would be back to sea.

Davey came down from the wheelhouse and went below to get his gear. Meanwhile Thomas and Paul finished up their duties and joined us. On the deck, there were other groups of friends waiting to get ashore. Several of the deck hands had to stay aboard to remove the hatch covers and then they could leave the ship.

"There's the *Anderson*," Paul said pointing to the *Arthur M. Anderson*. "Two of our roommates are on that ship. We'll have full house tonight."

"I can stay aboard," Davey said. "Nonsense, we've got plenty of beds as long as you have good lungs to blow them up," Thomas said.

We pulled up at the dock and waited until the ship was tied up and the gangway was lowered. Then we filed down to the dock. We looked up in the wheelhouse and Captain McSorley nodded to us with a smile.

"He's sure a nice man," Thomas said.

"You've got that right," Davey said. "I've been on a few ships where the captain was like a tyrant. Captain McSorley is really a fair and good man. We're lucky to be with him."

We all piled into our car which we'd parked at the back of the lot at the dock and headed to the room. When we walked in the door the two guys from the *Anderson* were happy to see us.

Thomas introduced us to Brandon and Levi.

"We saw you coming into the harbor so we took the liberty of purchasing a couple of boxes of fermented malt beverages."

We all had big grins as we each opened a cold brew and put our stuff into the closet. We sat and talked and drank beer with our two new friends for a couple of hours until our beer ran out. Then we decided to go and visit Henry and see what he was up to.

Brandon and Levi had their own car so Paul rode with them and we all drove over to Henry's place. He was in the driveway with a big cooler sitting on the ground and the grill smoking.

"Let me guess," I said, "You saw us come into the harbor and knew we'd be thirsty?"

Henry was grinning. "You might say that. I figured you'd be ready for some red meat burned over charcoal too."

He opened another smaller cooler and it was half full of pieces of chicken, small rib eye steaks and some brats.

"Holy smokes Henry," Mark said, "you must have been expecting an army."

"More like a navy," he replied. "Help yourselves to a beer and one of you can help me grill this stuff. The rest of the feast is in the house so a couple bring it out and we'll eat in a few minutes.'

Two hours later we were all stuffed and getting a little silly with the beers. I'd slowed down since I was driving and Levi also had switched to soda. We shared stories with our two new friends and Henry told us of some of the tales of his days at sea.

It was a glorious afternoon. Henry seemed to be very happy to have us there. We finally decided it was time to go back to the room. I quietly took up a collection from the others and we left $40 under a plate on the table to help pay for the groceries and beer. We knew if we tried to give Henry some money he wouldn't take it so this was a way to get him to accept it.

"We're leaving late tomorrow for Detroit," I said to Henry. "We've got to wash clothes tomorrow so we'll probably be back in about 6 days."

"I'll keep the home fires burning," he said.

We left Henry in the driveway waving to us. I felt a little sad seeing him there alone. We were lucky to have made friends with a great guy like him.

We were all full of food and nearly full of beer when we got back so we all decided to go to bed. We had to blow up 3 air mattresses and that took a lot of laughing and goofing around. When we finished we had wall-to-wall beds.

Tigger sat on top of the refrigerator and watched us. She had a look on her face that seemed to say, "Silly humans".

The light was just starting to shine in through the windows the next morning when the first fart sounded. It came from somewhere to my left. Soon another blasted into the silence and then another from the other side.

"Jeez, what a bunch of pigs," Thomas growled from his upper bunk.

One of the guys let three quick farts in response to his growling.

Then Thomas turned his back to us and blasted one of his giant thunderbolts. It didn't take long for the rest of us to vacate the room.

"Dang, that guy is dead inside," Levi said.

"Especially after beer, he's just unbelievable."

A while later after we'd all gone to the bathroom, we made a big breakfast of scrambled eggs and bacon and toast. Then we all loaded up and drove the two cars to the Laundromat and washed clothes.

The rest of the afternoon we spent just laying around talking. The *Anderson* wasn't leaving until the next day so they said they'd take care of filling Tigger's bowls. We bid our new friends goodbye and drove back to the ship. They were just starting to lower the hatches back over the holds when we came onboard. By the time we got our gear stowed we were underway. Mark and I walked up on deck and looked toward the shore. We could see Henry sitting in his chair on the fishing dock near the beach where we'd caught the smelt. We yelled and waved.

Henry looked around and then saw us and waved back.

"Kinda like an extra grandpa," Mark said.

I nodded in agreement. We turned to go down to the galley to start work and Mark stopped. He pointed to the west. There were big black thunderclouds roiling off in the distance.

"Looks like a storm is coming," he said.

"It looks pretty nasty, we might have some rough weather."

A little less than an hour later we found out just how rough it was going to be. We were helping Alan and the ship began to roll and pitch.

Alan looked up at the ceiling. "Must be getting rough up there," he said. "We'll have to be careful down here. We don't want to be wearing any hot food if we get rocking and rolling."

The storm must have been really strong because the ship began to buck and roll very sharply. You nearly had to hold onto something to walk from one end of the galley to the other. It was pretty hard to work but we managed until Mark started to turn a light shade of green.

"You gonna be sick?" Alan asked.

"Dunno, I'm feeling a little whoosey," he replied.

"Go and sit down and if you feel sick do it in here," Alan said handing Mark a bucket.

Mark sat in the corner on a bag of potatoes and soon he had his head in the bucket.

Alan looked over and grinned. "Rookie," he said.

Chapter 25

The storm seemed to grow and the lake became even rougher. It was difficult to stand without hanging onto something in the galley. Part of the crew came down to eat and the rest stayed on duty to keep everything going right in the storm. When the first bunch of sailors had finished they went topside and the hands that were working came to eat.

"We'll fix some plates for the bridge," Alan said.

So he and I fixed three plates of food for the captain, first mate and Davey who were all on the bridge of the ship. We filled a thermos with coffee and put the whole works into a container that was for just this type of situation. Mark and I walked to the front of the ship on the port walkway under the deck to deliver the food. We came out on the deck and climbed the stairs to the bridge.

The wind was howling and waves were crashing on the side of the ship throwing up sheets of water across the deck. The waves looked huge, maybe fifteen feet tall. Mark and I had to hang onto the stair railing just to keep from falling as we tried to climb to the bridge.

"Dang, it's terrible out here," Mark yelled over the wailing of the wind and the sound of waves breaking against the ship.

"Let's get up there quick," I said urging him upward.

We dashed into the bridge and the officers were happy to see us. The captain told the first mate and Davey to eat and he'd handle the ship while they did. We stood to the side to watch the wild water outside the windows.

"Is this normal?" I asked Davey.

"Well it happens. I've seen it worse than this a few times, but not many. Thankfully I've never been in any worse."

"We're having winds to at about 35 knots so that's a pretty good storm," Captain McSorley told us.

"What exactly is a knot sir? I asked.

"A knot is a unit of speed equal to one nautical mile which is 1.852km per hour. In layman's terms it's about 1.15 miles per hour. So 35 knots is about 40 miles per hour."

Just then a huge wave slammed into the bow and covered the windows with water and foam.

"That was a good one," Davey said. "These windows are 20 feet above the waterline so that was a big wave."

"Are we in any danger?" Mark asked.

"As long as our engines keep running and we have steering we'll be fine," the captain said. "This ship is well built and we do know what we're doing don't we John," he said to the first mate.

"Aye sir, we've made it through ugly weather every time."

"John and I have sailed together for a long time. We made a pact years ago to stick together until we retire or die on the sea," the captain said.

"And at the age we're getting, I think that retirement is looking pretty good... one of these days," John said.

"Not right away, but one of these days," the captain added.

They grinned at each other like old friends often do.

The rain was beating against the windows and the noise was very loud in the bridge. John finished his meal and Mark got the captain's meal and he sat at a small table and began eating. Davey finished his and put his dishes into the container.

"Good stuff," he said wiping his lips on a napkin. "You guys make a couple of good assistants for Alan, he's a darn good cook but he needs good helpers too."

"Thanks he's fun to work with," I said.

The rain seemed to be slowing a bit. There were still flashes of lightning now and then but the storm seemed to be subsiding. By the time the captain finished his meal the wind was slowing.

"It looks like the worst is over," he said bringing us his plate. "David, you can stand down now. I think John and I can handle it. The night watch will be here in a short while and if the storm quiets down we'll turn it over to them. Mike and Mark, thanks for the good meal. It was much appreciated."

We picked up the dirty dishes and Davey walked with us back on the under deck walkway back to the galley. Alan had most of the food put away but there was a stack of dirty dishes and pots and pans to wash.

"Take off," I said to Alan, "we'll clean up."

"Are you sure?" he asked.

"No problem. We'll handle it," Mark said.

Alan grinned and hung up his apron. "See you in the morning."

I began to fill the sinks and Davey rolled up his sleeves and put an apron on.

"You don't have to help," I said, "you're an officer."

"I'd rather help and have somebody to talk to when I get back to our quarters than go back there and have nothing to do. Besides, I'm just a student really. It'll be a long time until I become a real officer."

We all pitched in and cleaned up the galley and when we were walking down the hallway to our quarters we ran into Thomas and Paul coming off their watches. We decided to play poker for a while before bed.

"Pretty bad storm," Thomas said. "Did any of you landlubbers feed the ducks?"

I grinned and pointed at Mark.

"Get a little sick?" Paul asked grinning.

"No I got a lot sick," Mark said.

We all had a good laugh. A couple of hours later we decided it was time for bed so Paul and Thomas left and we each undressed and got into our beds.

"Captain McSorley and John have been together a long time?" I asked Davey in the low light coming in through our porthole.

"Yeah, I think they've been together for many years. They've said many times they'll sail until they either get too old and have to retire or until they go to the bottom together."

I had no idea that in just a few months that is exactly what would happen.

Chapter 26

We went on to Detroit and made a pretty fast turn-around. The ship was unloaded and we cast off and headed back for Duluth the next morning. We spent a day crossing Lake Huron and toward evening another storm blew in from the west. This one wasn't as bad as the first one on this trip but it was pretty windy and made the lake rough.

The next morning we were about half an hour from the Soo Locks and Mark and I walked up to the wheelhouse after we'd cleaned up the breakfast dishes. Davey was driving the ship. He had a huge grin on his face as we walked into the wheelhouse. John was sitting at a chart table drinking coffee and reading a book.

"Are you sure you know where you're going?" I asked.

"I think that's Spain up ahead there," Davey said.

John looked up and shook his head and went back to his book.

"Are there any helmets available?" Mark asked.

Davey just grinned and flipped him a bird.

We walked up by Davey and looked out over the lake. It was pretty rough this morning. The sky was dark and filled with black clouds and the wind was coming from the northwest.

"Looks like it's going to be stormy again today," I said.

Davey nodded, "It sure does. Those waves are getting pretty big, they look like 6 footers now."

It was pretty tense as we approached the Soo locks but Davey managed to get us through without hitting anything. He was smiling pretty wide as we sailed out into Lake Superior.

It was getting windier as we went farther north.

"The storm is building," he said.

Suddenly Mark pointed to the north. "Look there, is that a fishing boat?"

We all looked where he was pointing and at first I couldn't

see anything but finally I saw splashes as waves slammed into the small boat crossing in front of us.

"He's out a long way," Davey said. "We must be four miles from shore. He's probably trolling for lake trout." Then he shook his head. "He should have gone in before it got so rough, he's in trouble."

John got up from his book and walked up by us.

"Keep an eye on him," he said. "Make sure you steer well away from him but watch to make sure he gets into shore as long as you can see him."

Davey acknowledged he understood.

The boat was now about a mile in front of us and to the right of us. He was really taking a beating from the big waves. He'd go down in a trough and we'd lose sight of him and then he'd come up on the crest of the next wave and disappear into the next trough.

"I'd hate to be in that little boat," Mark said.

"It's probably not such a little boat," I said. "It looks like it's probably an 18 or 20 footer. In calmer water it's probably a very safe boat but in this weather it's not big enough."

The boat went down into the next trough and we watched expecting it to come up on the next crest but it didn't appear. Davey turned to John, "I think he swamped John!"

John came running. He grabbed the handle and cranked it to All Ahead Slow. Then he called the engine room, "Just keep us moving boys, we might have to rescue someone."

When the next wave swept past where we'd seen the boat we could see it in the water upside down. There were two guys clinging to the bottom. Suddenly one of them went under water.

"Holy smokes he's gone!" Mark said.

The guy was gone for what seemed like many minutes and suddenly he came back up with something in his arms. He made his way up to the side of the boat and a small black and white dog climbed up onto the upturned bottom of the boat.

"He went down to get his dog, oh man," Davey said.

"David, sound the horn so they know we see them, then steer close but don't run them over."

"John, maybe you should do this, I'm not sure..."

"David, you can do this, I have to get the crew on deck and alert the captain. Just watch and take your time. You two help him." And John left the wheelhouse.

Mark looked at me. "Oh great, a cadet and two cooks driving a 700 foot boat."

Davey turned around and looked at him. "Well, you wanted the excitement of the sea," he said.

The men in the water waved at us and Davey tooted the horn again to let them know we saw them. Then he eased the ship forward ever so slowly.

We looked down from the wheelhouse and saw some of the deck hands lowering a cargo net over the side.

"They can climb up that net," Davey said.

"What about the dog? He can't climb it and those guys can't climb with a dog in their arms."

Davey looked worried. "You better run and mention that to John."

Mark ran down the stairs and we could see him talking to John. John shook his head and looked around trying to figure out what to do.

"The swings we used for painting," I said.

"Good idea," Davey said, "you better run down and tell John your idea."

I ran down to the deck and told John what I'd suggested to Davey. He grinned at me.

"That's brilliant, who's going over?"

"Well," I said, "since it was my idea, I guess it should be me."

"Mike you're scared when you sit on a bar stool," Mark said.

"Well there's no better time than the present to get over that fear," I said.

We ran to the storage closet and got one of the swings that we'd used to lower over the side when we painted the scrape on the ship's side. I looked over the side and we were getting very close to the upturned boat.

"John, let's get it over and then if you get five or six of the deck hands, they can lower me down and then, hopefully, pull me and the dog back up.'

John nodded. "Mark run up and tell David to take her two degrees starboard and dead slow."

Mark ran up the stairs and disappeared into the wheelhouse. I looked over the side again and we were within fifteen feet of the boat.

"I'm coming over with a swing. When I get down hand me the dog and then you guys climb up the net," I yelled to the two fishermen.

They nodded and waved.

Five of the deck hands gathered and we put the swing seat over the side. I took a deep breath and grabbed the rope and lowered myself down to the seat. John watched over the side.

"Are you okay?" he asked.

I nodded. I was too terrified to speak.

"Okay, lower away, slowly boys."

Chapter 27

The swing was a two-foot long 2x6 pine board with a hole drilled about an inch from each end. A length of sturdy rope ran down one hole, under the board and up through the other hole back up to about three feet above the seat where it was tied back around itself.

I clutched the knot so tightly that my knuckles turned white. The ship was rolling because of the six-foot waves so the seat was swinging to and from the ship. The farther down from the railing that I got, the more the seat swung. I chanced a peak over my shoulder and the upturned fishing boat was right below me. The waves were pushing it toward the *Fitzgerald* and as they slammed into the side of the ship they splashed ice-cold water up at me. One second I was ten feet above the boat and then a wave hit and I was only 4 feet above it. They lowered me a little more and the next time we went into the trough, I went into the water and then was pulled up again as the ship rode up the wave. I was shaking like a leaf. The water felt like I'd been stabbed with a thousand little needles.

The crew had dropped the cargo net over the side and it was hanging into the water next to me. The two guys in the water looked terrified. They were both probably in their late 20's and were shivering badly.

"Can you climb up that net?" I asked them.

"I think so, but what about him?" one of the guys said nodding to the little dog.

"I'll take him up."

"Ok, because I'm not leaving him behind," the guy said.

"Don't worry, we'll get him up."

The guy on the side of the upside down boat that was closest to the ship grabbed a handful of net and let loose of the boat. He struggled to get a foot into the webbing but soon made it up out of the freezing water. Meanwhile waves were crashing into us and I was drenched with frigid water that felt like ice.

Once the first guy was partway up the net he stopped and hung on for a minute. His legs were shaking probably as much from the cold as from the fright of being dumped into Lake Superior. Then he started climbing again. I motioned to the other guy to hand me the dog.

"Hand him up," I said.

"Buster, come on kiddo, let's go," the guy said to the little dog.

I looked at the little dog and he looked like he was about ready to give up. He was shivering and looked about half dead.

"Come on Buster," I said holding out my hand.

The dog looked up at me and back at his master. The guy lifted him up and I grabbed him behind the front shoulder and lifted him up into my lap. A wave hit us just then and I almost lost him but held onto one leg. He scrambled back up into my lap and looked up at me with terrified eyes.

"It's ok little guy," I said as quietly as I could. "You're ok now."

He just looked at me and shivered.

The second guy on the boat worked his way around to the side of the boat next to the *Fitzgerald* and then began climbing up the cargo net. He stopped and looked back to make sure Buster was okay.

"I've got him, don't worry," I said.

I looked up at the railing of the ship and saw Captain McSorley looking over the side. "Are you ready?" he asked.

I nodded. I'd been hit by many waves and was drenched to the bone. The cold water was seeping into me and I began to shiver just like Buster was shivering.

"Hold on little guy," I said, "we're going to get up there and get warm."

The dog looked up at me and blinked several times and then burrowed into my lap as deep as he could go. He was shaking like a leaf.

The captain turned and said something to the crew and they

began pulling the rope over the railing. Buster and I rose up out of the splashing waves. I looked at the little guy and realized that he was a Boston terrier. He had the classic black coat with white forelegs and a white chest and neck with a white stripe running down between his eyes. His flat little face and big eyes gave him kind of a look like those English bulldogs but on a smaller, cuter scale. He was shivering and clung to me for dear life.

"It's okay little guy, you're okay now," I said.

He looked up at me and licked my chin.

When we got to the rail I handed Buster off to one of the deck hands. Then two strong crewmen grabbed me by the shoulders and hoisted me over the side onto the deck. My legs gave out from under me because I was so cold and I flopped onto the deck like a dead carp. One of the deck hands helped me up. The two fishermen were wrapped in blankets waiting. The owner of the dog wouldn't leave the deck until he knew his little buddy was safe.

"Take them down to sickbay and have the Third Mate check them over," Captain McSorley said. The Third Mate was our unofficial doc. He had EMT training and was as close to a medical person as we had aboard. He and several deck hands helped the two guys up to their feet and steadied them to help them walk to sickbay. They were both shivering badly and pretty worn out from being in the water for so long.

"I'll bring him down as soon as we get him dried off and warmed up," I said to reassure the fisherman.

"You guys will take care of him?" the captain asked.

"Aye sir, we'll get him warmed up and maybe get him a bite to eat. He'll be fine."

Mark and I started for the stern to our quarters and the captain stopped me.

"Good job," he said smiling.

"Thank you sir," I said.

We took Buster to our quarters and got a big towel and dried him off. It didn't take much since he had such short hair. He was still shivering and Mark pulled a blanket off the bed, took his shirt off and held the dog in his arms next to his bare chest. Then wrapped the blanket around them both so he'd get warmth from Mark's body. I stripped my wet clothes off and dried off with a towel and then dressed in my heavy sweats.

Buster was peaking out from the blanket and seemed much happier.

"He's kind of a cute little guy," I said petting the side of his little face.

"The face only a mother could love," Mark said.

"Oh that's not so, he's... well, okay, he's not beautiful like a golden retriever but he is cute."

After a while Buster began to squirm like he wanted to get out of the blanket. Mark put him on the floor and he began to explore our room, his little docked tail just wiggling back and forth. We decided to take him to the galley and see if Alan had anything for him to eat.

"I'll feed him," Alan said. "Warm up a little milk and give it to him to heat up his insides."

While Buster was drinking his milk, Alan warmed up some beef and gravy and set it down for him. Boy to say he was hungry was an understatement. He wolfed the food down and then licked the bowl until there wasn't an atom of food left.

"I bet he'll feel better now," Alan said.

We decided to go see how the fishermen were getting along. Mark carried Buster to the sickbay and when we walked in both of the guys were sitting on chairs wrapped in blankets drinking coffee.

"Buzzman!" the fisherman said. Buster jumped in his lap and he hugged the dog.

"Thank you so much for saving him," the guy said amid much wiggling and licking from the dog. "I thought I'd lost him when we capsized."

"We saw you dive down under the boat and had no idea what

111

you were doing," I said.

"We went over so fast I didn't have time to grab him. But the boat has flotation and there was an air pocket up under the hull. I hoped he had been able to get to that air pocket and when I went down for him he was dog paddling around under there. He was pretty darn happy to see me."

Alan came in with two big bowls of hot chili and gave it to the guys.

"This'll warm up your inside," Alan said.

"There is no doubt you'll warm up with that," I said. "No doubt."

The guys began to eat and one looked up with tears in his eyes. "Wow, that's got some spunk to it!"

Buster was trying to get into his master's bowl so the guy finally scooped up a little chili in his spoon and let the dog have it. He licked the soup off the spoon, licked his lips and then sneezed.

"I think he likes it," the guy laughed.

Chapter 28

"I'm Doug and this is Steve," the fisherman said. "We're brothers-in-law.   We're married to twin sisters.   Quite a coincidence isn't it?"

"Yeah, twins seem to be a part of your life," I said.

The two of them were wrapped each in a blanket and from what we could see that's all they were wearing. Steve left a bit of chili in his bowl and set it down for the dog to finish. He licked and licked until it was sparkling clean. Then Doug did the same and Buster finished his chili too.

"He likes people food," Doug said.

"I can see that," Mark replied. "I hope the chili won't upset his stomach."

"Oh it probably will. He'll be a fart machine in a little while."

We laughed. "He farts a lot?"

"Yeah, with that short nose they gulp a lot of air when they drink and eat and they're well known for passing gas. When we first got him, my wife almost took him back when he began farting in bed with us. We got kind of used to it. In fact it works out pretty well for me, I can slip one out now and then and blame it on Buster and I get away with it."

We thought that was pretty funny. "Poor Buster," Mark said.

"What were you guys doing out so far from shore?" I asked.

"We were trolling for lake trout," Doug said. "Several years ago I worked with the fishery people and the University of Wisconsin surveying spawning reefs for the lake trout.   I actually worked for them for 4 years and we mapped the lake floor and found many natural spawning reefs. We made maps with the coordinates of the reefs. That was before Loran C came to be but now Steve and I have them programmed into our Loran, well our now drowned Loran. Once we get out here, we put in one of the reefs as a waypoint and then go and troll over it back and forth.   It's a lot better than just fishing blind and usually pays off with some nice trout."

"We saw the waves were getting big but we were on some fish and hated to leave," Steve said. "We paid for that mistake."

"Well, boats can be replaced, but luckily you got rescued and are safe now," I said.

Buster had crawled up on Doug's lap, nestled there, snoring up a storm. We looked down at the little guy.

"He's quite a pup," Mark said.

"Oh that he is," Doug said smiling at the dog. "He's just all personality. My wife would have left me if he'd been lost," he said. "I'd sure have missed the little guy too."

Just then we heard a little toot and a blast of horrid air hit us.

"Jeez, he unloaded one already," Steve said fanning himself.

"Do you want to take him with you for a while?" Doug asked.

"No way," I said, "but thanks anyway."

"We have to get down to the galley and help get lunch ready. I expect you'll have to ride with us to Duluth. Why don't you go up to the wheelhouse and talk to the captain, I'm sure he'll fill you in on what's going on."

They agreed to do so and thanked us again for helping to save them. Mark and I went to the galley and began helping prepare lunch.

A while later when we had the food ready the crew began filing in to eat. Captain McSorley arrived with our guests, including Buster, and they ate with him and the officers in the second dining room. Their clothes had been dried and they were looking pretty good for taking a swim in the lake.

Thomas was sitting next to Paul eating and when he looked up he had a surprised look on his face. "Doug! What the heck are you doing here?" He exclaimed.

Doug was equally surprised to see Thomas. "Holy smokes, Tom how the heck are you?"

They embraced like old friends. "My friend Steve and I are the two knuckleheads who capsized their fishing boat and were rescued by your fine ship and Captain," he said.

"I heard we'd rescued some guys but I was working in the engine room. I had no idea it was someone I knew," Thomas said.

"How do you two know each other?" Mark asked.

"We worked on a lake trout project one summer," Thomas said. "We mapped the reefs and stocked lake trout fry."

Doug nodded. "Tom and I spent hundreds of hours under the water mapping reefs. We spent a little time quenching our thirst after the dives too." He grinned at Thomas.

"So let me guess," Thomas said, "you copied the maps we made and you were fishing the reefs for Lakers."

Doug grinned. "There's nothing wrong with a little knowledge when it comes to finding fish."

"Why don't you get your food and then you can sit and catch up on old times," I said.

Doug and Steve filled their plates and then sat across from Thomas and we all shared some of their stories about their lake trout adventures.

Davey walked into the dining room a bit later and we introduced him to the guys and let him in on the coincidence of Doug and Thomas being old friends.

"We're about two hours from Duluth," Davey said. "We've called ahead and let their wives know they're with us and they're going to be waiting for them to pick them up. The Coast Guard is sending a cutter out to see if they can tow their boat in."

"So all's well that end's well," Mark said.

"Yup, they were pretty lucky we happened by when we did or they'd have died from hypothermia. It doesn't take long in that cold water."

"Brrrrr," I said. "I'd hate to have that happen."

"They say it's not so bad," Davey said, "I've heard you just get real sleepy and drift off."

"I guess that wouldn't be so bad, but still… " Mark said. "I'd hate to find out if that's true."

Chapter 29

The harbor was very busy when we got to Duluth. There were ships being loaded with grain and taconite and one with scrap metal that was going to be melted down to make new cars. There was a ship ahead of us and we met three leaving as we got close to the harbor.

"This is a busy place," Doug said. He and Steve and Mark and I were in the wheelhouse so they could see how the ship was handled going into the dock. Davey was at the bow thruster and John was steering while Captain McSorley oversaw the whole thing.

"This is the 11th largest port in the world," the captain said. "Over 1,100 ships use this harbor every year and that's during a 10 month time period. There are two months a year when it's frozen over with ice."

"Where do they all come from?" Steve asked.

"They come from all over the world," the captain answered. "That one there," he said pointing to a ship being loaded with grain "is from Russia. Those two over there are from Norway. It is 2,300 miles from here to the Atlantic Ocean. That's through all of the great lakes and the St. Lawrence Seaway to the shore of the Atlantic. Then it's 2,300 miles across the Atlantic to Europe. So once those ships leave here, they've got a 4,600 mile journey."

"That's pretty amazing," I said.

We were moving very slowly toward the Burlington Northern Dock and when we got close Steve went to the window and began waving to two women on the dock.

"That's our wives," he said smiling.

"They look mad," Doug said.

"Yeah, we're probably gonna get an ass chewing," Steve added.

Mark grinned. 'They're not happy with you?"

"Well they always kind of gripe when we take off fishing and now that we've done this, we're going to have to do a lot of shopping and husband stuff to get them over their mad," he said. "They'll come around when they see Buster."

At the sound of his name, Buster woke up and started to stretch. Then he farted.

"Who did that in my wheelhouse?" Captain McSorley barked.

"It was the dog," I said.

He looked at the little guy wagging his little stub of a tail. "If you were a human I'd make you walk the plank little man."

Buster stood up on his hind legs and licked the captain's hand.

"We'll be tied up soon. I hope you gentlemen have luck getting your boat back in service."

"We can't thank you enough Sir," Steve said. "We owe you our lives."

"We were happy to help," the captain said. "The boys will help you onto the dock. Calm seas."

Thomas met us on deck and we walked the guys to the gangplank that had been lowered to the dock.

"Once the wives cool down and we see if we can get our boat going again, we'll call you guys and maybe we can set up a time for a fishing trip. That's IF you trust us not to capsize you," Doug said laughing.

Thomas and Doug hugged. "It was sure good to see you again, even if it was under kind of bad circumstances. I hope we can get together and go out and see how those Lakers are growing later in the summer," Thomas said.

"You can count on it," Doug said. "It'll take us a while to get the boat going again but once that's done and the wives cool off, we'll get in touch with you. We'd love to have Mike and Mark and Davey come too."

'We'd like that too," I said.

"Cool, it'd be a good way to pay you back for all you guys did for us." Doug said.

"Well, good luck with the wives."

"Thanks guys. We'll never forget the *Fitzgerald* and the crew. You'll always be in our prayers."

We all shook hands and hugged. Doug wrote down our phone number and we hugged Buster goodbye. We watched as their wives hugged and kissed them and made a big fuss over Buster.

"Well, I think we've made some new friends," I said to Mark.

"Yeah, I think you're right. Let's go see if Paul and Davey are about ready and we can go back to the room and have some barley pop."

I grinned at my brother.

"You're getting to like that stuff pretty well," I said.

Mark just grinned.

Chapter 30

Henry was sitting on the bottom step of the stairs up to the "Dump" and had a big grin on his face when we drove up. '

"I saw you guys coming into port so I thought I'd see if you're busy tonight," he said getting a hug from each of us.

"What ya got in mind?" Thomas asked.

"Well, I got into a nice mess of northern the other day. I caught three of them and the smallest was almost fifteen pounds. So, I thought some deep fried fish and potatoes washed down with a little soda or something would be nice. That's *if* you guys don't have something better planned."

We all looked at each other. "I can't think of much that would be better than a fish fry and a few sodas, as long as there are *Barley Pops*," Mark said.

Henry grinned from ear to ear. "Now that's what I hoped you'd say."

We put our gear into the room and spent some time with Tigger and then cleaned up. Mark and I went with Henry to begin getting the food ready and Thomas and Paul went to the beer store and got some refreshments.

An hour later we were feasting on deep fried pike and potatoes and washing it down with some cold beer.

"Henry every time you cook fish for us I think it's the best fish I've ever tasted and then the next time you cook some that's even better," I said.

"Northern is a fine eating fish," Henry said. "You have to know how to get the Y bones out of them and once you do that, they're excellent eating. A lot of people don't know how to clean them and so they throw them back. They don't know what they're missing."

He was certainly right about that. We ate until we were ready to bust. Then we cleaned up the dishes and sat in lawn chairs looking out at the lake.

"So how was your voyage this time?" Henry asked.

We told him about rescuing the fishermen and one of them turning out to be Thomas's friend.

"So you were part of that lake trout project?" Henry asked.

"Yeah, I spent one summer working on it. It was a good job but I was under water most of the summer."

"I heard about it," Henry said. "Do you suppose it's going to do any good?"

Thomas shrugged. "I've heard they're finding more and more lake trout in different year classes, so they must be spawning."

"So just what did you guys do?" Paul asked.

"Well, its kind of long story," Thomas said.

Davey looked in the cooler. "We've got enough beer for quite a while."

We all laughed.

"Okay, well, it started quite a while ago. There used to be many lake trout in both Lake Superior and Lake Michigan and they began to dwindle in numbers after World War II. People were over fishing them and then in 1959 the St. Lawrence Seaway opened and that almost spelled the end of them. Along with a route to and from the Atlantic for ships, another critter used the canal... the lamprey. They found their way into the great lakes and decided they loved attaching to lake trout. In just a few years the numbers of Lakers dwindled to a very low number.

In 1970 the University of Wisconsin started a project to study the problem and try to come up with a solution. I worked on Lake Superior on a small boat called the *Dawn Treader*. This was in the days before Loran C so there was no really accurate way to map the lake. We used small transponders called mini-rangers and placed them at different locations on the shore in different areas to find the coordinates of spawning reefs. These little transponders would send out a signal about 2 miles. We'd go out in the boat and dive to the bottom and look for reefs. When we found one we'd send up a buoy and the *Dawn Treader* would take readings from the three signals from a receiver on the boat and triangulate the signals to find our latitude and longitude. Then they'd record it along with the depth, and size and shape of the reef. We spent hundreds of hours mapping reefs up to 80 feet deep."

"So what is Loran C?" I asked.

"That's right you guys are from farm country aren't you?" Thomas said grinning. "Loran C is a new system that the government has installed. They built huge antennas all over the country and each one of them sends out a signal at the same time. Instead of the little portable mini-rangers, you now can triangulate on three of these antennas to find your latitude and longitude anywhere in the country and most of the world. Each signal goes out at exactly the same second. Then your Loran unit receives the three signals and the time it takes them to get to the unit can be computed to latitude and longitude by a computer in the machine."

"Why only to 80 feet?" Mark asked.

"Because if you dive to 80 feet or more you can only stay down a short time or you have a serious chance of getting the bends. It was about the maximum depth we felt safe for the project."

"Okay, I understand that. I've heard the bends are pretty bad," I said.

"Oh, you have no idea," Thomas said.

"You got the bends?"

Thomas nodded. "Big time."

Chapter 31

"We'd been diving about 10 hours a day for nearly two weeks and we were in an area where we were just about at the maximum depth for diving. I came up after mapping a reef and when I got into the boat my skin felt like I had ants crawling all over it. It was the beginning of the bends, probably caused by so many days of diving in a row. They took me to shore and an ambulance was waiting that took me to a Coast Guard helicopter. They flew me to Milwaukee where they had a decompression chamber. I was in misery and the pilot and corpsman couldn't do much for me except try to keep me comfortable.

We tried to land on the roof of the hospital but it was really windy and we just about crashed, so the pilot radioed he was taking me to a park nearby. It was one of those big soccer parks where there are soccer fields all over the place. We landed on a vacant one and they carried me out on a stretcher and put me in the shade of a tree waiting for the ambulance to take me to the hospital.

I was laying there pretty much in misery with my eyes closed. The pilot and corpsman were there with me and pretty soon I heard other voices. I opened my eyes a little and there were about a hundred kids surrounding us looking at me on the ground.

I closed my eyes again and then a bit later I heard a little voice.

"Hey mister."

I opened my eyes and this little black kid was staring at me. "What?" I said.

"Are you from outer space?"

I frowned a bit and then I realized I was still wearing my bright red dive suit with all kinds of gauges and valves on it. I grinned and looked at him and said, 'Take me to your leader.'

The kid's eyes got as big as golf balls and he took off like a shot"
We all laughed at Thomas' story.

"So the bends are pretty bad?" Mark asked.

"Bad enough," he said, "I'd never want to get them again. They're one of the hazards of diving in a deep body of water."

"The lake is one of the deepest lakes in the world," Henry said. "It's the third largest in the world by water volume."

"So how deep is it?" I asked.

"The deepest place is 1,332 feet deep, about a quarter of a mile."

"Wow, I'd hate to fall in there," Davey said.

Henry laughed. "Anything over about 6 feet deep will drown you Davey, the other 1,326 feet is just added bonus."

"The reason it's so much deeper than the other lakes is that about a billion years ago two previously fused tectonic plates split apart. The immense weight of the ice from the glaciers was so great that the crust of the earth couldn't support it. A valley was formed providing a basin for what eventually became modern Lake Superior. Then at the end of the last glacial period about 10,000 years ago, the melt-water filled all of the lakes. Because of the uneven nature of glacier erosion some of the higher hills became the Great Lake Islands. They've sent mini-subs down in that deep valley and the walls are nearly vertical. It shows that the crust of the earth just split apart from the huge weight."

Thomas spoke up. "Do you guys know what a drumlin is?"

Davey said, "It's like a pile of debris left by a glacier I think."

Thomas nodded. "When a glacier moves across the land the debris that is left behind is called glacial drift. It consists of all of the rocks and boulders that have been ground along with the ice and eventually get deposited in places along the way. Glacial drift is why there are no caves in the northern part of Wisconsin. When the glaciers came along they filled all of the caves with rocks and boulders. In the southwest part of the state where Mark and Mike live there were never any glaciers.

There were 4 ice ages and each one of them missed that part of the country. That's why it's called the Driftless Area. A drumlin is just a long sloping pile of that glacial drift. If you drive across northern Wisconsin or the other northern states, you find the land is pretty much flat with slightly undulating high spots. Those high spots are drumlins, piles of rocks and boulders deposited by the ice. Through rain, wind and farmer erosion many of them are just gently undulating little hills.

He looked at Mark and me. "Where you guys live there are big tall hills that tower over the valleys and are much different than the north. The only caves that we have in the northern part of the area are caves along the coast of the lakes that are formed by water and waves."

"When you're on the bottom of the lake, you can see the piles of rocks as they were 10,000 years ago when they were left there. It's pretty cool, like stepping back 10,000 years in history."

"Wow that sounds cool," Mark said.

"If you guys want to, we can do some diving on some of the reefs when we get together with Doug. He has them mapped and I know he has scuba gear."

"We've never dove before," I said.

"I can teach you. We won't go out in 80 feet right away, we'll start in shallow water and work our way down."

"Cool," I said.

Davey walked over to the cooler and got a sad look on his face. "The cooler is empty," he said.

"Time to go home," Henry said.

"Or to the beer store," Thomas said.

Thomas had the better idea for sure.

Chapter 32

Henry looked like he was ready to go to bed so we thanked him for his hospitality and headed back to our room. On the way we stopped and got another box of beer.

We all settled in and opened a cold one and Tigger hopped up on Mark's lap and curled up for a nap.

"So, is it pretty cold under the water in the lake?" Davey asked.

"Darn right, it's only about 34 or 35 degrees," Thomas replied. "In the summer the surface temperature might get up to 60 degrees which is pretty darn cold. But from January to June and then again from November to January the surface temperature is only between 38 and 40 degrees. Not what you'd call swimming temperatures. We wore heavy insulated suits but even so it was pretty cold. You get used to it after a while though. Doug was a good diver and a lot of fun to work with. We spent hundreds of hours together under the water and in a motel during the rest of the day. He was always good for a prank too. Once when we were mapping a reef he went down the side a little way and was out of sight. Suddenly I looked up and there was a shark coming up over the reef."

"A Shark! In Lake Superior?" Davey asked.

"Doug had a rubber shark hat that he'd snuck down with us. He put it on his head and then swam up toward me. I about crapped my wetsuit."

We all had a good laugh picturing Thomas' encounter with a shark. "So did you see any sunken ships?" Mark asked.

"No we didn't, and I thought we would. There was a barge at one reef and a few small boats but no big ships."

"There have to be lots of them out there," I said.

"There are about 350 known wrecks dating way back to the 1600's," Thomas said.

"Wow, that's a lot. Why so many?"

"Well, it's a big lake and in the months of November and December, storms come through that cause huge waves. Of course some of these wrecks were because of fires or exploding boilers, but many were sunk by gale force winds."

"That's scary, but a ship like the *Fitzgerald* would be pretty safe compared to those small ones," Davey said.

"I'm sure the size of the *Fitzgerald* makes it much safer than a small ship but any ship that is made out of steel and iron will sink."

"So the storms get pretty bad in November?" I asked.

"Winter storms can be terrible. They come out of Canada and bring lots of wind and sometimes snow and sleet. They've taken many ships to the bottom."

Davey looked uneasy. "We won't be still hauling ore that late will we?"

Thomas shrugged. "It depends on the weather and if the ice begins to form I suppose. I wouldn't worry Davey, the *Fitz* is built like no other and has all the best equipment in the world. I think we're as safe on her as we are right here in this dumpy room."

"Well, I don't know about you guys," I said, "but I'm ready for bed. We have to report back aboard at noon tomorrow, so I think I'd rather do it without a hangover."

Everyone agreed so we drank up and all used the bathroom and in a few minutes I turned off the lights and crawled into my bunk. I watched as Tigger leapt from the floor to the dresser to the top bunk. I heard Mark talking to her as she most likely snuggled with him. It didn't take long for me to fall asleep.

Chapter 33

We reported to the ship on the last day of September. Mark and I decided that we'd take off the first semester this fall and return to school for the second semester in January. That way we could finish out the season on the *Fitzgerald* and spend a little more time with our new friends.

It was quite surprising what good friends we'd become with Thomas, Paul and Davey. We all especially liked Davey. At first he seemed kind of awkward and a loner but we soon found that he was a great guy and a great friend.

"I've never had such close friends," he told me once. "I've always been kind the odd guy out. When my friends were chasing girls and playing football I was studying marine laws and reading books on the great sailing ships. I kind of got used to being a loner but you guys have been so nice to me... its just really cool to be one of the guys."

We were sailing to Cleveland this trip so we'd be gone a couple of extra days. Mark and I reported to the galley and began working on the evening meal. Thomas and Paul went to work and Davey reported to the bridge. Captain McSorley had promised him that he was going to let him steer the ship out of the harbor. He was pretty excited about that.

We'd been in the galley for over two hours when we felt the vibration of the engines running. That meant we were soon going to be leaving the dock. We had nearly everything ready for dinner, the bread was rising in pans, the beef roasts were seasoned and oven ready and the potatoes and vegetables were ready to be cooked.

"Hey Alan, is it okay if we go up on deck for a while?" I asked. "Davey's driving out of the harbor and we'd like to watch."

"Sure, we're good here. I'm going to take a nap anyway. Come back about 1600 and we'll get everything in the ovens."

Mark and I took off our aprons and climbed up to the deck. It was a glorious fall day with the sun shining and a slight breeze off the lake. There were deckhands casting off the lines from the dock and we could see Davey up in the front of the bridge standing at the wheel, ready to steer the boat.

I waved to Davey and he waved back but looked nervous. "He looks scared," I said to Mark.

"I'd be scared too," he replied, "it's got to be terrifying to steer this big thing."

Soon we could see the bow thruster pushing us out away from the dock. It took several minutes to get us far enough; Davey gave three toots on the horn and then the propellers in the stern started pushing us forward.

We looked up and Davey was intently watching everything around him making sure not to run too close to any other ship or dock. He was doing great and we had to smile when he looked down at us and grinned.

We were out a quarter of a mile into the harbor and all seemed to be going well. Mark and I laid back on one of the hatch covers and closed our eyes and soaked up some sun. We hadn't been napping long when I heard the horn sound long and then it did the same thing again.

I sat up and looked around. Up ahead of us coming out from the backside of a long grain dock was another ship. It was steaming forward and seemed not to have seen us heading for it. I looked at the name, *SS Hochelaga.*

"That guy is coming out right into our path!" I said to Mark.

We looked up and could see Davey turning the wheel frantically. We got closer and the other ship didn't seem to realize we were there. Davey blew the horn again and again.

The *Hochelaga* must have finally seen us because it began to turn away from our path.

"It's turning!" I yelled.

"It's not going to make it," Mark replied.

He was right, we were headed right into the port side of the other ship and nothing was going to change that.

Chapter 34

We were standing at the rail just below the wheelhouse and could see the starboard side bow thruster was going at full speed. Water boiled out from under the bow but it was going to be too little, too late.

The crew on the other ship was watching us bear down on them and you could see on their faces they were terrified. Suddenly one of them yelled something and they all scattered toward the bow and stern, away from where a seven hundred foot behemoth was about to ram into them.

The captain came out of the under deck stairway and looked across the quickly narrowing gap between the two ships. He shook his head and ran up the stairs to the wheelhouse.

We were still turning but time had run out. We hit the side of the *Hochelaga* about one third of the way back from the bow. There was a tremendous bang and then we felt the tremor of steel on steel shudder through the *Fitzgerald.* Our ship was three times the size of the *Hoclelaga* so we kept moving ahead and the other ship was pushed away like a toy. In just a few seconds it was turned almost completely sideways and up against the end of the dock. We felt the engines reverse on the *Fitzgerald* and could see that we were slowing down.

Captain McSorley came from the wheelhouse and looked across at the other ship.

"Was anyone hurt that you could tell?" he shouted to us.

"No Sir," I said, "they scattered pretty fast when they saw we were going to hit them."

The Captain grinned. "I expect so," he said. "Please stand by in case we need any help."

We nodded that we certainly would.

The Captain went back inside and we could see him talking on the radio. A minute later we saw a man wearing a captain's hat hurrying to the wheelhouse of the *Hochelaga*.

"Somebody's gonna get an ass chewing," Mark said.

"No doubt."

Many of our crew was now on deck and we all went forward to see if the *Fitzgerald* had been damaged. We looked over the side and could see a bunch of paint scraped off the bow but not much more damage was obvious.

"Nothing a couple of buckets of paint won't fix," the third mate said grinning.

"I bet that guy driving the other ship about crapped his pants when he saw us coming," one of the crew said.

"He must have been sleeping, it'd be pretty hard not to see a ship this size bearing down on him," the mate said.

Just then Davey came out of the wheelhouse looking a little shaken. He stood there looking across the water at the dent in the side of the other ship and then he looked down at us. He shook his head and grinned.

"Are you done being the driver?" I asked, trying not to grin.

"You'd think so wouldn't you?" he answered. "But the captain of the other ship just radioed... the guy driving was listening to his walk-man full blast with head phones. He was grovin' to the tunes and didn't hear the crew yelling at him to get out of the way. I think he may be done driving though."

We all laughed and were glad it wasn't Davey that was going to have the blame on him.

He came down the stairs and we all gathered around him. "Jeez, I don't know if I'm cut out for this," he said.

"First I ran into the Soo Lock, now I hit another ship."

"You must be cursed," Mark said grinning.

"I must. But thankfully the Captain isn't angry with me. But he did mention that when we get to Cleveland I should spend a little of my time on re-painting the bow."

He looked expectantly at us.

"We'll have it done in no time and still have time for a few brewski's on shore," I said.

Davey was grinning from ear to ear when he heard that.

Chapter 35

We had to wait for the Coast Guard to show up and investigate the accident. They had people board each ship and question the people who'd been on the bridge. Davey and John had to each pee in a cup to make sure they weren't on drugs. By the time they were done on the *Fitzgerald* they had a harbor tug tied up to the big dent in the *Hochelaga* and an engineer looking at the damage. The bow of the *Fitzgerald* had pushed the side of the other ship in about a foot but the metal hadn't split apart so it was probably still seaworthy.

Finally a call came from the Coast Guard that we could be on our way. Captain McSorley's voice came over the loudspeaker that the show was over and that everyone should go back to his duties. We all began filing back down the deck to our jobs. We'd wasted about three hours with the crash so it was time to feed the crew dinner. Mark and I joined Alan in the galley and baked our bread and put the roasts in the oven and made ready for the crew to eat.

During the next hour or so the crew filed in and ate their dinner. Davey came in near the end and filled his tray. He was sitting alone at the table, so Mark and I walked over and sat with him.

"So Crash, how are you doin?" I said grinning.

Davey shook his head. "Jeez, can you believe it? There's a three hundred foot boat ahead of me and I run right into it. I'm lucky I'm not down here peeling potatoes."

We laughed. "It wasn't your fault," Mark said.

"Probably technically it wasn't," Davey said, "but still, like they say on Hee Haw, 'If it weren't for bad luck, I'd have no luck at all.'"

"I'm sure Thomas and Paul will help with the paint job when we get to Cleveland and we'll have it all done in no time. We'll still have a whole day to spend on shore."

Davey grinned. "I'll probably get thrown in jail again, knowing my luck."

"We'll take special care of you. If we see you going after a girl who has a boyfriend, we'll just throw you over our shoulder and haul you out of the bar."

"Okay, that's a deal," he said.

Davey went back to the bridge and we cleaned up the dinner dishes. We didn't have anything to do until 600 hours so Mark grabbed our camera and we walked up on deck to take some pictures. We'd been on the largest ship on the Great Lakes for many weeks and had nothing to prove it. We took pictures of the deck hands, the bridge from the stern of the ship, and one of Captain McSorley standing on the landing of the bridge looking out over the lake. We got a good one of Thomas scratching his head trying to figure out why one of the machines in the engine room was malfunctioning. Paul was sacked out in his bunk, snoring with his mouth hanging open when we took a candid photo and I got a good one of Davey at the wheel, steering the huge ship.

"I'll get these developed when we get back to Duluth," Mark said. "They'll be something to look back on when we're all old men."

The rest of the trip to Cleveland was uneventful. Davey drove through the Soo Locks with nary a scrape and the Captain even let him drive when we tied up at the dock.

He was grinning pretty wide when they shut down the engines.

The crew made everything shipshape and started opening the hatch covers so the ore could be unloaded. Thomas and Paul came on deck where Mark, Davey and I were getting the swing seats and ropes ready for our painting job.

"You know, I'm the one who crashed," Davey said, "you guys don't have to help."

"Open the paint, Short Crotch," Thomas said.

I volunteered for one swing seat and Paul took the other.

The other three lowered each of us down over the bow and then lowered a can of paint to each of us. We began painting the bow where we'd hit the other ship.

"I wonder how many times crew members have done this?" Paul said as we hung there slapping paint on the huge steel monster.

"It looks like there are quite a few coats of paint," I said. 'I doubt that's the first time this old girl has run into something."

The sun was shining and the breeze was very comfortable. We were suspended about 30 feet off the water. We finished the first two pails of paint and they hauled us up onto the deck. Thomas and Mark went down and we lowered them about 5 feet lower than Paul and I had been. In no time we had the job done and we all were cleaning up the brushes and putting the gear away.

"So, I guess I owe you guys a beer," Davey said wiping his hands on a rag.

"I'd say so," Thomas said.

"Well, let's see what we can do in Cleveland then," Davey said leading the way down the gangplank.

We found a bar that served Mexican food not far down the street and went in and began drinking some Mexican beer. It wasn't long and we had to throw down a shot of tequila and after that, things got hazy.

Chapter 36

We'd been in the bar drinking mostly beer and an occasional shot of tequila when we decided we were hungry. Thomas went up to the bar for a menu and we decided on the "Twenty Taco Plate".

"Serves six to eight people, can be ordered mild, hot or fiery," Thomas said reading the menu.

"Fiery for sure," Davey said taking a big swallow of beer.

"Are you sure little man?" I asked. "These Mexicans really mean it when they say something is hot."

"I love hot food... and hot women," he replied looking around the room.

"Oh jeez, not again," Paul said.

We calmed Davey down and ordered the Taco special with the fiery sauce, and another round of Mexican beer.

The place was filling up and soon there were three other sailors at the next table. They said hi as they sat down and we struck up a conversation with them.

"So what ship are you on?" one of them asked.

"We're on the *Edmund Fitzgerald*," Davey said, "I'm the maritime cadet."

"Wow, that's quite a ship, ours is much less impressive but she's a good ship," one of them said. "We're on the *Carl D. Bradley.*"

"What do you carry?" I asked.

"Mostly grain and corn," was the answer.

Our tray of tacos came and the waitress sat it in the middle of the table. She was a hot little gal with black hair and eyes and a definite curve. She flirted with us as she passed out single plates to all of us.

"Holah," Davey said. "You mucho prettio."

The girl shook her head. "Keep an eye on your little friend," she said grinning, "I think he has too many beers."

We assured her we would keep Davey safe and sound. We all grabbed a taco and began eating. The conversation was over for a bit as we all chomped into our tacos with gusto. I'd eaten about a half of mine when I started to feel the burn. The sauce was sweet and tangy and didn't seem very hot... at first. But then a minute later I began to feel a burn deep in my throat and it worked its way up into my tongue and lips. My eyes began to water and I could feel sweat breaking out on my forehead. I looked across the table and the other guys were also looking a little distressed... everyone except Davey.

"Wow! These things are as advertised," Thomas said taking a drink of beer.

Paul didn't say a word. He just grabbed the water pitcher and began drinking right from it. "Mama mia" he gasped.

The guys at the next table were laughing like mad at our discomfort.

"Looks like you bit off more than you can chew," one of them said.

"These are great!" Davey said reaching for another taco.

We all just looked at him as he stuffed the thing in his mouth like it was a Twinkie.

"Don't you think those are a little too spicy?" Mark asked.

"I told you I like spicy food."

We ordered more beers and offered our new friends a taco. They all took one and found them pretty spicy just like we had. Everyone was eating slowly and drinking a lot of beer or water between bites, except Davey. He stuffed taco after taco into his mouth and then guzzled more beer to wash them down.

The tray had just two tacos left when Davey announced he needed to hit the bathroom. He stood up and kind of stopped and shook his head his eyes fluttered and then fell over backwards right onto the middle of our new friends' table, out like a light.

We all jumped up to make sure he wasn't dead and found him snoring heavily with a stupid grin on his face.

"Poor little guy, he just overdosed on tacos and Mexican beer."

We decided to finish up and head to our rented room. Thomas called a taxi and we all went out to the street to wait for them.

"So you guys going to be here for a while?" one of the other guys asked.

"We're leaving tomorrow afternoon," I said.

"So are we, we're headed for Duluth to pick up a load of corn."

"That's where we're headed too," Paul said.

"Maybe we can meet up in Duluth and have a little party," Mark said.

The new guys thought that would be a great idea so we gave them our phone number in Duluth and our address. Our taxi pulled up and we all piled in. It was a full cab with the five of us in it but we made it to the room. We carried Davey up the steps and Paul and Mark pulled off his shoes and socks and pants and we put him in one of the bottom bunks with a trash can next to him in case he needed to blow up during the night.

Then we all bedded down with burning throats and rumbling stomachs.

Chapter 37

The air in our room smelled like a giant taco fart. We all felt pretty bad and smelled worse, except Davey, he was all chipper and ready to go.

"You guys just don't know how to party," he said as he emerged from the bathroom wrapped in a towel.

"Do me a favor and shut the hell up!" Mark growled.

"Oh don't be such a baby, get up and let's get going, we're heading back to Duluth today and I plan on driving part of the way."

"Well if you run into another boat today, you're doing your own damn painting," Paul said.

It took a while for everyone to get going but eventually we were ready to go back to the *Fitzgerald*. Captain McSorley was standing on the deck by the bridge watching us file aboard with a grin on his face.

"Morning gentlemen," he said, "you look like something coughed up by a seagull."

We had to laugh. That's exactly the way we felt.

Soon we were underway. I looked for the *Bradley* but didn't see her in the harbor. They were probably on their way north already.

We made the uplake trip with no problem. Davey didn't run into anything and the weather was beautiful. Mark and I spent as much time as we could on deck enjoying the mild temperatures and slight breezes. It was much nicer now than when it had been so hot earlier.

As we pulled into Duluth harbor I saw the *Bradley* tied up already at their dock. I looked carefully but didn't see any of the guys who we'd met the previous night.

When all of our duties were done we all walked down the gangplank for a two-day layover with instructions to be back at noon on the second day.

"So, should we stop at the beer store?" Davey asked excitedly.

"Jeez, we've turned you into a monster," Thomas said, "But since you mentioned it, I am a bit thirsty."

"Since it's so nice, let's see if Henry's around and maybe have a cookout at his place. I hate to stay inside in Chez-Dump on such a nice day," I said.

We decided that was a good idea so we not only got some beer, we also got some brats and hamburger and the fixings. When we got to the Dump, we were surprised to see two of the guys from the *Bradley* walking down the stairs from the upstairs landing.

"Hey, there they are," one said.

"Hi guys, what's up?"

"We thought we'd come over and see what you guys are up to tonight?"

"Well it just so happens that we've just come from the beer store and market and are going to have a cookout on the beach," I said.

"Oh, well, maybe we can get together tomorrow," one of them said.

"Why don't you guys come with us? We've got plenty."

"Sure, that'd be great. Say, we don't even know you guys names and you don't know ours."

We found out that the tall dark haired guy was named Trent and the shorter lighter haired guy was Eric. They were both 22.

We stowed our gear in the room and all piled into the car and drove to Henry's place. It was a tight fit with seven of us and all the food and drink but we made it. Henry was sitting on the front driveway when we drove up.

"I was wondering if you guys were going to show up," he said grinning.

"We're having a barbeque unless you've got other plans," Mark said.

"Well, I'll have to give my tickets to the opera to someone but I think I can attend your little gathering. We seem to have two more in the party too."

We introduced Henry to the two new guys and began getting things arranged for the cookout. We knew our way around pretty well so we just told Henry to sit and chat with us.

It didn't take long for the smoke to begin rising from the grill. In no time we had everything cooked and were sitting around Henry's picnic table eating.

Henry was regaling everyone with stories of the high seas when Eric asked him if he knew the story of the Ghost Ship, the *Bannockburn."*

"I think everyone who sails Lake Superior knows of it," Henry said. "Why do you ask?"

Eric looked uncomfortable. "I think I saw it last night when I was on watch."

Henry's eyebrows went up. "Do tell," he said.

"Henry what's this about?" I asked.

"It's an old story, a ghost story about a ship that was lost 73 years ago," he replied.

I looked at Eric, "And you think you saw it last night?"

Eric nodded.

Chapter 38

I looked over at Thomas, Paul and Davey and they looked concerned.

"Oh come on... you're not going to tell us that a ship that sunk over 70 years ago is still sailing out there are you?"

Thomas shrugged. "Sailors are the most superstitious people in the world."

"The *Bannockburn* has been a bad luck omen for decades," Henry said. "It's reported to be out there haunting other ships."

"Here, pull my other leg, it plays Jingle Bells," Mark said sticking his leg up on the table.

Henry grinned. "You guys are still landlubbers, you don't know about all the stories of the sea."

"Well, then enlighten us," I said.

"The *Bannockburn* was built in 1893 by a British shipbuilder. She was 245 feet long and was one of several British ships on the Great Lakes delivering cargo to American ports. She was named after the location of the mighty battle of 1314 in which Robert the Bruce won independence for Scotland from England."

"I read about that guy in world history class," I said.

"Well then you know things didn't turn out too well for old Robert. They tortured him to death but he did what he set out to do, free Scotland. Anyway on November 22, 1902 she left Port Arthur in Ontario with a belly full of grain bound for another Canadian port. Late in the afternoon the *Algonquin* passed her near Isle Royal. The captain of the *Algonquin* said that the *Bannockburn* was in plain sight when she suddenly vanished without so much as a sound. He turned his head for a second and when he turned back the other ship was gone.

Later that evening the passenger ship *Huronic* also reported seeing the *Bannockburn* noting her telltale three masts against a backdrop of a brewing winter storm. She was reported overdue later that night as the winter squall churned up the water.

There were sightings that placed the ship at half a dozen different places at the same time during the evening. Relatives of the crew claimed they received telegrams from their loved ones on board telling them not to worry and assuring them that the ship was safe and on course.

The storm made it impossible to launch a search right away. It was later in December before divers took to the water to search for the wreckage. They came up empty. To this day not a single piece of the ship or any evidence of it has been recovered. It simply vanished from the face of the earth. But, occasionally other ships still see the three masts in the distance as the Ghost Ship sails even now."

We were all sitting slack jawed as Henry finished his story.

"Well, that's kind of spooky," Mark said.

"So you're telling us that this ship is still out there 70 years later and if someone sees it they're jinxed?" I asked.

"I just relayed the story. You can take for what it's worth," Henry said.

"You're not worried about it are you?" Mark asked Eric.

"I saw a three mast ship, that's all I know."

We sat there for a minute and Davey got up for a beer. "Well, we might as well enjoy ourselves. You never know if your time is up on this dang lake."

That seemed like a good enough excuse for another beer.

We finished up the beer and cleaned up the meal leftovers and thanked Henry for his hospitality. Then we dropped the guys off at their ship and went back to the Dump.

We were all pretty tired so we went right to bed. Tigger jumped up on Mark's bunk and he snuggled her to his chest.

"How does she know which one of us she's snuggling with?" I asked.

"I must smell better," he said.

Chapter 39

The next day we were loaded and set out on a downlake trip to Detroit. We steamed past the *Bradley* and Trent and Eric were on deck securing hatch covers. They waved to us and we waved back.

"I wonder where they're going?" Mark said.

"We'll have to watch for them in Detroit and maybe we can get together with them. They were pretty cool guys."

"You know," Mark said. "I've been thinking that we've learned a lot and met a lot of really cool people this summer. I think that skipping one semester was a good idea even though Mom and Dad weren't real excited about it."

"Practical knowledge is sometimes better than what you learn in books," I said.

"Plus we've met some great guys. I expect we'll all be friends for the rest of our lives."

The journey to Detroit was pretty uneventful. During the hours when we were off watch we got together with the guys and played cards and watched TV and had a lot of fun just talking and joking.

At Detroit we went to a movie and had some pizza. We were told that we should report back to the ship early because we were doing a fast turn-around. On the way back to the harbor we saw the *Bradley* was tied up two docks down from us so we walked over to see if Trent and Eric were on board. We asked one of their mates and he said they'd gone ashore so we left word with him to tell them we'd stopped by.

The unloading didn't go as fast as planned so we went downtown and had some Chinese food and then headed back to the ship. The *Bradley* was just pulling out of the dock when we walked up.

Trent and Eric were on deck tightening down the hatch covers and we yelled at them. They waved to us.

"Are you going back to Superior?" Trent shouted.

"Yeah, how about you?"

"We're going to Manitowoc. This is our last trip. Do you guys care if we come up to Superior and visit?"

"No problem, come any time. We'll have a party."

They were all grins as we waved and walked to the ship.

"The weather is getting bad," Mark said as we walked aboard.

I looked at the sky and it was all black and full of big rolling clouds.

"The gales of November," I thought to myself.

We went to work while the crew got us underway. By the time we had dinner ready the ship was rocking and rolling pretty well. The crew came in a few at a time because it was safer not to leave any station unattended in weather like this. It took longer than usual to feed everyone but we finally did and began to clean up the galley.

"Gonna be a wild night," Alan said.

"We'll be okay though?"

"Oh sure, this is a good boat, she'll hold up," he said.

"I wasn't too worried about us," I said, "I was thinking about the *Bradley*. We're a lot bigger than she is. We have a couple of friends on that ship."

"If it gets too bad the captain will take them close to shore where the wind will be less of a threat," Alan said. "I wouldn't worry; these captains have a lot of experience."

We took the under deck walkway up to the bridge. When we came on deck to climb up to the bridge the wind was really blowing and the lake was churning up and blowing sprays of water across the deck. We hurried to the bridge and found Davey steering.

"Oh that makes me feel real safe," I said when I saw Davey.

He grinned. "What? You don't think I can do it?"

"I'm just afraid you'll run into something," I said.

Mark began laughing. "Is there anything within a few miles of us?"

"In fact the *Bradley* is just ahead of us," Davey said pointing through the windows.

We looked and could barely see the ship pounding through the waves a couple of miles up the lake from us. They looked like a cork boat on a very violent pond.

"They're taking a beating," Mark said.

"I've called them a couple of times and they said they're okay," Davey said.

The second mate was also on the bridge and he was watching with binoculars.

"They're empty so they pumped 9,000 gallons of water into their holds for ballast," he said. "That should help them stay stable."

"It's getting pretty rough," I said.

"It's going to get worse," Davey replied.

Chapter 40

We decided to stay on the bridge. For some reason I felt safer watching what was going on than being in our room and not knowing what was happening. Weather reports kept coming from the radio and they were getting worse.

The forecast was for the 25 to 35 miles per hour winds to pick up to gale force of 50 to 65 miles per hour and change from southerly to southwesterly. Two weather systems were converging. One was a snowstorm in Nevada and the other a line of tornados from Texas to Illinois. Things were going from bad to worse.

About 4 pm the second mate called the *Bradley* to see how they were doing.

"We're riding comfortably with a heavy following sea."

Davey shrugged. "I guess he's okay," he said.

It was getting close to the time when Mark and I were going to have to go back to work when we heard, or more likely felt a thud.

"What the heck was that?" I asked.

"It didn't come from us," Davey said.

"It came from the *Bradley,* the mate said. "We felt it through the water.

"She's slowing down," Davey said.

We watched as the back half of the *Bradley* seemed to sag in the water. I looked at Mark and he looked frightened. "It looks like they broke in two," he whispered.

"Mayday, mayday, mayday... this is the carrier *Bradley.* We are dead in the water with catastrophic hull failure... Mayday, may..." The radio went silent.

I looked up at the radio and then back at the water and the *Bradley* was gone.

"Where did it go?" I yelled.

"Gone, it's gone," Davey said with an amazed look on his face.

The mate called the captain and in a minute he was on the bridge.

"Radio the Coast Guard, give them our position. Request assistance from any vessel in the vicinity. Get the lifeboats ready."

Since we were right there we put on rain gear and started out to untie a lifeboat.

"Be very careful out there. These waves will wash you right off the ship. We have enough people in the water without adding any of our own," Captain McSorley warned.

Mark and I held on to railings as we moved toward one of the lifeboats. We loosened all the clamps and hooked up the pulleys to lift it off the deck when we were ordered to. By now we were about where the ship had disappeared and expected to see men in the water and hopefully Trent and Eric. All we saw was some debris and a few lifejackets floating in the huge waves. A Coast Guard cutter showed up and began searching.

We were freezing as the wind blew waves across the deck soaking us even though we had on rain gear. Soon two more of our deck hands showed up to help us if we needed to lower the lifeboat but there was no one to save. They were all gone.

The Coast Guard radioed that they'd found a life raft with two men on it. A little later they found a man alive in the water but then reported he died after being pulled aboard.

That was it. In the next few hours there were 6 more vessels searching for survivors and not one was found. We stayed on the deck until the first mate came and ordered us inside.

We were both shaking from the cold and wet and he and Davey helped us get down to the walkway under the deck and to our room where we stripped and took hot showers and got warmed up.

"Alan is gonna kill us," Mark said when he noticed how late it was.

We hurried to the galley and found Alan working with Thomas and Paul.

"Davey told us you were on deck with the lifeboat so we came to help," Paul said.

"Any sign of Trent and Eric?"

I shook my head. "The Coast Guard found three guys and one was dead. No sign of Trent or Eric," I said.

We were all quite stunned. It isn't often that you see someone you know who dies right in front of you. While we didn't know these guys real well, we had enjoyed their company and hoped to have a long friendship. Now they were gone.

"Come and eat," Alan said. "We've fed everyone else."

We sat and ate a bowl of chili and finally got warmed up so we weren't shivering any longer. Thomas and Paul sat with us and we really didn't know what to say.

Finally Thomas said, "Remember Eric telling us he saw that Ghost Ship? That's kind of uncanny isn't it?"

I felt a chill run down my back. "That's just too strange," I said.

The rest of the night the wind blew and the waves pounded us. The captain stayed on the bridge through the night and so did Davey. When he came to our room in the morning he looked like a zombie.

"Are you okay?" I asked him as he sat on his bunk staring at the porthole.

"Yeah, I'll be okay after some sleep," he said.

"That's not something you expect to see," Mark said.

Davey nodded. "I guess it shows you how fragile life is on the water. One minute you're there, the next minute you're in the cold water at the bottom of the lake."

Chapter 41

The storm was still raging but we held our own. We stayed close to the Wisconsin shore so we were out of the wind somewhat. Mark, Davey and I slept hard and when Alan knocked on our door at 600 hours we were surprised the night had passed without any of us waking up. Mark and I got up to help with breakfast.

The talk in the dining rooms was of the loss of the *Bradley*. Everyone was stunned by the news and the normal laughter and joking was absent. We steamed into Duluth harbor about mid-morning and once all of the chores were done we were told that we'd have three days off. Our next trip was to Detroit at the end of the week and we were glad to have some time off to rest and to think about the loss of our new friends.

The five of us piled into our car and stopped for groceries and some beer. We stopped off at Henry's but he wasn't home.

"He's probably out fishing," Thomas said. "I'll leave him a note and tell him about the guys and that he should come over for supper if he wants to."

We went back to the Dump and the place was a mess. With different crews living there at different times it seemed that no one wanted to clean anything and it was getting pretty bad. Davey and Paul took all of the laundry to the Laundromat while the rest of us swept, washed dishes, cleaned the bathroom and even washed the windows.

There was a knock at the door and we expected Henry so I just yelled to come in. I was surprised when Doug and Steve walked into the room.

"Hey, we thought you were Henry," I said. Mark and Thomas were in the bathroom cleaning and came out to greet our friends.

"So what brings you to Duluth?" Thomas asked.

"Well it's suppose to be a nice weekend and with it getting

late in the season we thought it would be a good weekend to go out and do a little diving to see those Lake Trout reefs we told you about. If we find one with a lot of fish on it we can see if we can catch a few of them too."

That sounded like a good plan and we all agreed we'd like to try it.

"So your boat is back working?" Mark asked.

"Yeah, it cost a bit to get the engine overhauled but everything else dried out pretty well. Thankfully our insurance covered the costs so the wives are not as mad at us as they might have been."

"So where's Buster?" I asked.

"Oh he's in the pickup. We didn't know if you were here for sure so we left him there. Should we bring him up?"

I looked up at the top bunk and saw Tigger snuggled down in a nest she'd made in Mark's sweatshirt.

"I don't know how Tigger will like him but sure, bring him up. I'd like to see the little cuss again."

Soon Doug reappeared with the little dog and he went wild checking out all the new smells and wonderful things in the room. Tigger looked down over the end of the bed and if looks could kill, Buster would have been stone cold dead.

"Looks like Tigger doesn't like him much," Mark said. He walked over and picked up the cat and cuddled her. She meowed her displeasure. Buster heard her and was very interested in her.

"I think we better let her stay up there," I said, "Otherwise Buster might get a sore nose."

While we were talking with the guys about the fishing/diving trip Henry knocked on the door and we invited him in. He had a grocery sack with him and it had a bunch of food in it that looked like we were going to eat well that evening.

A while later Davey and Paul came back with the laundry and the Dump was pretty full. Henry suggested we go to his house and cook out instead of trying to cram so many people into our little place, so we all piled into our car and Doug's pickup and followed Henry home.

When we got there we all got together and helped get food and beer ready and an hour later we were all full of food and working on the beer. Buster galloped around the place and up and down the beach for about an hour and then he collapsed on Paul's sweatshirt that was lying on a chair and began snoring.

"So tomorrow we'll get the scuba gear out and go down to the beach and give everyone who wants to learn to dive a lesson in the shallow water. Then we can go out and locate some shallow reefs and take turns. We have two sets of scuba and several extra tanks.

Mark and I were excited about diving. Thomas had dived many times so he didn't plan on going but Paul wanted to try it too. Davey said he was a little uneasy about it so he decided not to go along either and would stay back with Thomas.

"We'll keep Buster with us so he doesn't get in the way," Thomas said.

I grinned at him. He liked the little dog and wanted to have him to play with him while we were gone.

We had to break out some of the blow-up beds later but eventually we all had a place to sleep. Buster was snuggled in Doug's arms snoring like a racecar. I was lying there smiling at how loud the little guy snored when I noticed Tigger sneaking down from Mark's bunk. She jumped to the counter and then to the floor. Then she walked very carefully and silently across the floor and sneaked up to the dog. She stopped and I could see her sniffing at him. She leaned in and smelled his face and then backed up and jumped up to the counter and then to Mark's bunk.

"What the heck was she up to?" I thought to myself.

I drifted off to sleep. The next day was going to be one that I figured would be one I'd remember for a long time.

Chapter 42

We followed Doug and Steve down to the lake and parked near the beach where we'd fished for smelt. Although it was late October it was a nice warm day so we wore swimsuits and tee shirts. Doug and Steve helped the three of us get into our wetsuits. They'd borrowed some extra suits from a friend of Thomas' so we all could go down together. They also had extra tanks, masks, and breathing equipment. It took Mark, Paul and me a while to get into the tight-fitting rubber suits. I even suggested we just swim in our shorts but Doug warned me that I'd be sorry for that if I tried it.

Once we were all dressed and in our gear we walked to the water's edge and put on our flippers. Doug showed us a few things about the mask and mouthpiece and then explained what we were going to do.

"You three just stay right between Steve and me. We'll wade out until the water is over our heads and then I want you to just bend down and look around. Take a breath through the mouthpiece and then just exhale as you do on land. After you're all comfortable with being under water, we'll swim out a little way and then when I signal, we'll dive down toward the bottom. You'll feel pressure on your ears but don't worry about that. "

"How deep will we go?" I asked.

"Just fifteen feet or so," Doug said. "We just want you to get used to being under water. Remember to exhale every time you inhale. The biggest problem many people have is that they hold their breath and get too much air in their lungs. Also once we're down a way, don't hold your breath as you swim toward the surface. It's very important that you exhale as your rise. The air in your lungs will expand as the pressure lessens near the surface and if you take a big breath at the bottom, you can explode your lungs by holding it all the way up."

We looked at each other and nodded.

"Ok, any questions?" Doug asked.

None of us had any so we waded into the water and soon we were neck deep.

"Just bend down and look around," Doug said and he disappeared.

I bent my knees and my head went under water. It was clear enough that I could see the others and the bottom. I inhaled and felt the air go into my lungs. It was kind of rush inhaling under the water. Then I made sure to exhale and take another breath. I was breathing a little fast, so I tried to calm down and soon I felt pretty comfortable.

I felt a tap on my shoulder and it was Doug motioning to me to follow him. I looked around and Mark and Paul were with Steve and were swimming out toward the deeper water and toward the bottom.

I nodded to Doug and together we swam out and down toward the bottom. The deeper we went the more pressure I felt on my ears and face. Soon we were at the bottom and Doug just motioned for me to swim around.

It was really amazing to be down on the bottom of the lake. The first thing I saw was an old beer can. Next a few perch swam up by me and I stopped and looked at them. I put my hand toward them and they moved back a little but didn't seem afraid of me. Doug and I swam over near the other guys and we all nodded and waved at each other. I could see Mark grinning around his mouthpiece.

Paul was swimming near the bottom and came up with an old tackle box. Doug gave him a thumbs-up and motioned for him to take it with him. We swam along the bottom for maybe a quarter of a mile along the beach. The bottom dropped off pretty steeply and we followed it down a little way until Doug motioned to come back up.

It didn't seem like very long and Doug and Steve began pointing toward the beach. We followed them back into shallow water and soon we were wading out onto the sand.

"What's wrong?" I asked as I pulled my mask off.

"Nothing is wrong. We've been under nearly 25 minutes. These tanks hold a half hour of air. We just didn't want to have one of you run out of air and panic."

"We weren't down there 25 minutes," Mark said. "No way."

Doug grinned. "Time goes past quickly. But yes, we were down that long."

The three rookies were all amazed. It seemed like we'd only been down for a few minutes. We walked back up the beach to where we were parked and took off the gear. Then we stripped off our wetsuits and piled them into Doug's pickup. We'd all brought extra clothes so we hid behind the pickup and stripped off our swimsuits and dressed in dry clothes.

"We'll take the gear up and dry out the suits and then we can go and fill the tanks," Steve said.

"Then first thing tomorrow, we'll put the boat in and go out and dive on a couple of reefs and see if any trout are living there," Doug added.

Steve got in with Mark and Paul and I rode with Doug to the dive shop to fill the tanks. As we were driving along we talked about the first dive.

"So was it what you expected?" he asked.

"I had no idea what to expect," I said, "but it was very cool. It's really quiet and peaceful down there."

Doug nodded. "It's like stepping back into history. Other than some beer cans and other garbage the bottom looks like it did centuries ago. It's pretty cool."

We stopped at the dive shop and while we waited for the tanks to be filled we walked next door and had a donut and coffee at a little shop.

"So when are you guys leaving for school?" Doug asked.

"Mark and I are going to skip the fall semester and stay on the *Fitzgerald* until her last run. We've learned so much and made such good friends that we decided it was the job of a lifetime and wanted to see it through."

"You won't have too many more trips this year," he said. "The weather is going to start to turn to shit and that will be the end of it. Usually about the middle of November is the end of the shipping season."

"Yeah, we figured that too. We'll finish up here and then take a little time off. We thought maybe we'd go to Florida and spend a little time before Christmas and then in January we'll be going back to school."

"Sounds like a good plan."

The tanks were filled so we loaded them up, stopped at the beer store and went back to the Dump. The guys were sitting and talking and Mark got my attention when I walked in.

"Look at the two friends," he said.

I looked and there on the bottom bunk were Tigger and Buster both curled up in a blanket sleeping together.

"She must have decided he wasn't so bad after all," I said.

Just then Buster lifted his head and yawned. Then he snuggled against Tigger and went back to sleep.

Chapter 43

The next morning the five of us got up early, and in a short time we were on our way to a boat landing to put Doug's boat into the lake and explore some reefs. We stopped at a diner and had breakfast and then backed the boat into the lake at a marina and once we had everything stowed away, we took off out to the big water of Lake Superior. Doug had his chart showing the reefs and their depth and he pointed to one that he thought would be a good one for us to dive on.

"This one is only a little over 20 feet deep at the top, so it should be a good one to look at first," he said. "That will give you three who are rookies at diving a chance to get used to being out in the middle of a lot of water."

The lake was pretty calm so we made good time as we motored out about a mile from shore. Doug turned on his Loran and soon we could see the reef coming up on the depth finder. Doug crossed it and Steve dropped a marker on the end of the rock pile. Then we turned and went part way around the thing and dropped markers on both sides and the other end.

"There, now we know right where it is," Doug said.

We all stripped down to our underwear and pulled on our wetsuits. Each of us helped another to get their tanks on and all the gear ready and soon we were ready to go into the water.

"Just stay with Steve and me and watch us for hand signals," Doug said.

We all shook our heads that we understood. Doug sat on the edge of the boat and went over the side backwards into the water. Paul went next and then Mark and I went after him with Steve bringing up the rear.

I righted myself when I hit the water and saw Doug swimming toward the rocks. I followed him and we all got to the bottom about the same time. The reef was exactly what I expected, a huge pile of rounded rocks that had been left behind by the last glacier as it passed over this spot. The rocks were exactly as they had been 10,000 years ago when they were deposited. Unlike glacial drift on land that got changed by rain and wind and farm machinery, this was undisturbed. On land farm plows, road-building machines, wind, and rain smoothed down the rock piles and sometimes obliterated them completely. But here on the bottom of the lake, the rocks were laying exactly where they stopped thousands of years earlier.

It was like being in a time machine and getting there just after the glacier receded. We swam around the top of the pile and then Mark and I swam toward the end and found it dropped off into much deeper water. As we hovered there looking down into the black water three large lake trout swam lazily past us just off the edge of the reef.

Behind them several more came swimming toward us. Mark pointed and I nodded that I saw them. He made a motion like he was fishing and nodded his head.

Doug swam up to us and waved. He motioned to follow him.

He took us along the edge to the north and soon we saw something much bigger than the rocks we were swimming over. Doug pointed and we looked at a large steel barge that was sitting on its side just at the edge of the reef. It was at least a hundred feet long and half as wide.

We followed Doug and soon we joined the others and Doug motioned for us to swim up to the top. When we broke the surface we took turns climbing onto the boat and took off our tanks.

"What did you think?" Steve asked.

"That was amazing. It looks like nothing has changed in many centuries," I said.

"That's right. The bottom of the lake looks just like it did ten thousand years ago. That barge hit the reef in a storm about twenty years ago and sunk. I thought it would be cool for you to see something like that too."

"It was," I said.

"There were some nice trout around the reef too," I said.

Doug nodded. "I've got another place a little way from here that I want to show you too. Then we'll be out of air and we can come back here and troll this reef and see if we can snag a trout or two."

We left the markers in the water and Doug fired up the motor and we headed up the lake. It all looked the same to me but Doug knew right where he was going and a quarter of an hour later we slowed and Steve tossed an anchor over the side.

"This is a cool thing but you have to be careful here," Doug said.

"What's down there?"

"When the country was just being built, loggers logged off the northern forests. The trees that stood on the shores of Lake Superior and the northern part of the country were cut and the lumber was used to build the cities in the new country. Chicago, Detroit, New York, and all of those cities were built with lumber that was grown here. It was all virgin timber. Trees that were standing on the shore of Lake Superior were saplings when Columbus arrived in the new world.

When they logged them, they floated them in the lake in huge rafts and down the lake to sawmills to be cut into lumber. They'd lash hundreds of logs together in a long string and then wrap that string of logs around a bunch of free-floating logs to keep them all together as they towed them to the sawmills. These rafts held thousands of logs and some of them got waterlogged and sank to the bottom. There was so much timber that they didn't bother about a small percentage of logs that sunk. This is an area that has thousands of those logs in piles and single logs lying all over the bottom. Some of these trees are extinct now and these logs are the only ones left of that species."

"Are they rotten?" Paul asked.

"No, they're as hard as the day they were cut. In fact they are even denser because of the time they've lain on the floor of the lake. Superior is so cold and there is so little oxygen at the bottom that there was no deterioration. These logs are in excellent shape and there are people starting to raise them and use them for fine furniture and other things. The wood is very valuable. It could be a huge business in a few years."

"Cool, let's go," Mark said.

"Just be careful. Sometimes the piles are solid and sometimes they're kind of haphazard. Don't get under any log that's in a pile. If it happened to fall on you, you'd be dead before we could find a way to get you out."

"Don't worry," Mark said. "I'll be extra special careful."

Chapter 44

We motored up the lake for twenty minutes and then Doug watched his Loran and when he found the spot he was looking for he motioned for Steve to drop the anchor. We all got our gear on and followed Doug to the bottom.

It looked like a logging yard back home. There were logs lying all over the place for as far as we could see. Some were just single ones and others were piled here and there.

"There must be thousands of them," I thought.

"I'd bet there are tens of thousands," Marks voice came into my head.

I looked up and there was Mark standing on a pile of logs waving at me. I went closer to some of the logs and marveled at how huge some were. There were many that were 4 feet across. I had no idea what kind of trees they'd been but there had been a lot of them and some must have stood on the shores of Lake Superior for several hundred years.

"Mike, look at this one," Mark's voice came into my head again. I looked and he was floating at the end of a log that was as wide across the end as he was tall.

"That must be 6 feet across," I thought.

Mark nodded.

We swam around the logs for a while and as I rounded a pile I saw a boat down in the deeper water out toward the middle of the lake. It looked like a tugboat of some kind. I swam over to Doug and pointed to it and he nodded. Then he shook his head.

I got the message that it was too deep, so I nodded. Doug pointed to the surface and we all started up. When we got to the boat we all climbed aboard.

"Leave your tanks on, we're just going a little way. I want to show you one more thing that's really cool."

They fired up the motor and we went north for a short way and stopped out from a point that ran into the lake.

"This is a really cool thing," Doug said. "We found this when we were mapping the reefs. This is what is left of a forest that once stood on the shore of the lake. At first when we found it we couldn't figure out how it got there but we contacted the Geographical Survey people and they looked at it. They decided that it was on the shore until the glaciers came and created the lake. The weight of the glacier was so immense that it actually depressed the crust of the earth. This shore that was once dry land was submerged and the forest is now below the surface."

We were all excited about seeing something like this and it didn't take long for us to get into the water and follow Doug to the bottom. He was right, there was a whole forest that followed the point out into the deeper part of the lake. The trees looked like they did centuries ago when they were submerged.

Doug kept checking his air gauge and soon he got our attention and pointed to the surface. We all followed him up and in half an hour we'd gotten out of our diving gear and into our fishing clothes.

"We cut it pretty close," Doug said. "I figured we each had about 5 minutes of air left. I wanted to get the most time we could out of the tanks for you guys."

We were all very appreciative for the dive and the amazing stuff we'd seen.

"Well, let's go and see if some of those trout are hungry," Steve said.

Steve began putting out lines with lures that would run at about 20 feet. We knew exactly where the reef was because we'd left our markers out, so all we had to do was to troll around the edge of it and hopefully a few trout would grab our baits. Steve had one line down and was setting another when the first rod began bucking.

"Fish on," he yelled. He looked at the three of us. "One of you grab that rod," he said.

We all looked at each other and finally Mark grabbed the rod and began fighting the fish. Steve didn't set the second line but kept it out of the water so it wouldn't get tangled with the one with the fish on it. He kept working on two more rods and watched Mark fighting the fish

"You're doing just fine," he said. "Just take it easy, they have soft mouths. Just pump and reel."

Mark fought the fish like a pro and soon we could see it flashing around behind the boat. Paul picked up the landing net and leaned out over the back and Mark led the fish into it. Paul scooped it up and soon it was flopping around on the deck of the boat.

"Nice one," Steve said, "That's about a ten pounder."

Doug was driving the boat and he told us to put the fish into a big cooler at the side of the deck. By the time we had all that done Steve had the first two lines back in the water and was setting the third. He'd just set it and the first one started bucking again. This time Paul fought the fish and it turned out to be a twin of the one Mark caught.

It only took ten minutes and we had another fish on the line. This time I had the fun of fighting it. This one was a little bit bigger than the first two and in no time we had over 30 pounds of lake trout in the cooler.

"That's some good fishing," I said to Doug.

"It helps to know where to fish and be able to dive and see if anyone's home," he said grinning.

We'd just rounded the end of the reef and suddenly two rods began bucking at once. Paul and Mark grabbed them and Steve hollered at me to help him reel up the other two. I grabbed the outside rod and began reeling and suddenly something slammed the lure and I was fighting a fish too.

Steve was laughing his head off. "Three fish on!" he yelled to Doug. Doug just stood there looking back and shook his head.

We were all fighting our fish and soon Mark's began heading toward the middle of the pack. He had to lift his rod up over Paul's head and follow the fish so they didn't tangle. His fish kept going and soon he was lifting his rod over my head and I was going toward Paul because my fish had headed that way.

"Holy smokes," I panted. "This is getting to be work."

We went back and forth several times and it looked like we were square dancing on the back of the boat. Suddenly Paul and Mark's rods went limp. Their fish had crossed each other and both lines snapped. I kept reeling and finally we saw my fish behind the boat. It was huge.

"Holy cow, that's a big one," Paul yelled.

He grabbed the net and I worked the fish close. Just as I thought it was over the fish dove again and my line snapped. I was pulling so hard I flopped over on my butt on the deck.

Doug and Steve were doubled over with laughter. "I knew it," Doug said, "I just knew it."

It was getting late so we put away the gear and headed into the dock. We'd had quite a day and it was one we'd not soon forget.

Chapter 45

The guys had strict orders to get home that night; even though we invited them to stay and have some beers and fresh lake trout they decided it best to get home to the wives.

"We're just now getting our "privileges" back," Steve said.

"We had to beg to bring Buster. They don't trust us after we nearly drown him."

We assured them we understood.

"So how much longer will you be on the water?" Doug asked.

"We could be finished any day," Davey said. "Right now we have two more trips planned. If the weather stays mild we'll go for a while yet but I doubt we'll still be making trips after the first week of November. I've heard the storms in November can be huge and there aren't many captains that will chance getting caught in one of them."

"Well, you guys have a good end to your season. Maybe next spring we can all get together and do some more fishing and diving," Doug said.

He and Steve said their goodbyes and they packed up Buster and drove off.

"They're good guys," Mark said as we watched them drive away.

"Yeah, we made two good friends when we happened across them that day," I said.

Paul and Mark drove over to Henry's to see what he knew about cooking lake trout and soon they came back with the news that we'd hoped for.

"Henry says the best way to cook lake trout is in a fish boil. He's got the gear to do it and he gave us a list of stuff we need."

We were all really hungry so we piled into the car and stopped at the market and got the stuff Henry wanted and then stopped at the beer store and got a couple of boxes of beer. Davey was grinning all the way to Henry's house.

"What's so funny?" I asked him.

"Oh nothing's funny, I was just thinking of opening a cold one and having a feast and thinking how much fun this summer has been."

"We have had some good times," I said.

"It's the best summer I've ever had. I hate to see it end."

Henry was waiting for us and had his fish boil rig all set up in the sand off the side of his driveway. He had a pile of firewood under a tripod that held a tall metal cooking pot that was suspended from the tripod. The pot was ¾ full of water that was steaming.

"What do you need us to do?" Mark asked.

"A couple of you can clean those vegetables up and chop them into bite sized chunks. A couple can clean two fish. Take off the heads and fins, then cut them into two inches thick chunks. The last one can help me get the fire built up."

We split up and Paul and I took care of the vegetables. We had rutabagas, carrots, onions, potatoes and cloves of garlic. It didn't take long to get them cleaned and chopped up. Meanwhile Davey and Mark got the fish ready while Thomas and Henry stoked up the fire and put the beer into coolers.

Henry took the rutabagas and carrots and dumped them into the pot. He let them cook five minutes and then put in the potatoes and five minutes later the onions and garlic. The smell coming from the pot was fantastic.

"Okay, now the fish goes in," he said.

He dropped the chunks of fish into the pot and had us lay many layers of newspaper on the picnic table. We got out butter and two big loaves of French bread. Then we watched as Henry took a jar containing a little gas and dumped it on the fire. There was a whoosh and the fire flared up, causing the pot to boil over.

"What the heck was that all about?" I asked stepping back.

"Lake trout are pretty oily fish so that oil is floating on top of the water. When we boiled it over it pushed all of the oil over the top and makes the fish a lot better eating," Henry said.

The boil-over nearly put out the fire, which was expected. Henry had Thomas take the pot from the tripod with a pair of heavy mittens. Then he lifted an inside pot which was full of holes up from the main pot and let the water drain out. Next he dumped the whole thing out on the newspaper.

There lay a feast. The whole pile was steaming in the cool evening air. The vegetables were all cooked and the fish was done to perfection. Henry took a dish with ground pepper in it and dusted the food liberally and then did the same with salt. We all sat down at the table and began picking up chunks of this and that and eating like a bunch of Vikings. It was an amazing meal and one we'd long remember.

"Henry, you outdid yourself with this feast," Thomas said.

Henry smiled. " It's always nice to have hungry people to feed, and I've never seen guys your age that weren't hungry."

We ate until there was just a scrap or two of food left on the table. Then we rolled up the papers and the "dishes" were done. Then we got serious about taking care of the beer. We didn't want it to spoil after all.

Paul volunteered to drink pop so he could drive home and we spent the rest of the evening laughing and talking.

"We better enjoy this night," I said. "It won't be long and the weather will be cooling off and the outdoor parties will be over for the year."

"I hate to think of the summer ending," Davey said. "It'll be the end of our friendship,"

"Why do you say that?" Thomas said.

"Well you guys will go back to school, and I'll have to make new friends next season on the ship."

"That doesn't mean we can't all get together during the summer sometime," Paul said.

Davey looked sad. "I hope that's true, but I doubt it will happen," he said.

Chapter 46

We left port in Duluth on November 1ˢᵗ with a load of taconite bound for Detroit. The weather had cooled off but it was a beautiful fall day as we passed out of the harbor. Davey was in the wheelhouse and Mark and I were working in the galley preparing the evening meal.

At dinner time the crew filed in and ate. When they were nearly finished Captain McSorley and Davey came in to eat. Davey looked a little worried but didn't say anything.

First Mate John was in the wheelhouse driving the ship and after they'd finished eating the captain returned to the bridge and Davey stayed behind.

"You look worried," I said as I cleaned up the galley.

"I am worried," he said.

"Why?" I asked grinning.

"The captain told me he wants me to drive tomorrow when we go through the Soo Locks again."

"You did okay last time," I said.

"That was going up the lake, this is going down the lake."

"So what?"

"Going down is harder. You come in at a steeper angle and you know how that worked out the last time I tried it."

I began laughing. "You smacked into the wall," I said.

Davey nodded. "Not funny," he said.

Mark came over by us. "So we can expect a collision tomorrow?" he asked.

"Oh you're real funny," Davey said. "But just in case, I'd wear a hard hat around mid-afternoon."

That night Thomas and Paul came to our room and we all played poker and laughed and talked late into the night.

Mark and I got up early to help with breakfast. Davey was still sleeping when we left. He came into the galley and had his breakfast and waved to us as he left.

"We should go up on deck and give him some moral support," Mark said.

I nodded. "Yeah, we'll clean up after lunch and then go up and watch the show."

We arrived on the forward deck just as the Soo Lock came into view. Davey was at the wheel driving the ship and he looked down at us and shook his head. We grinned up at him.

Mark and I stood on the bow as we approached the lock. While the space was massive, so was the bow of the *Fitzgerald*. There was enough clearance on the sides but any mistake could end up with the ship hitting the wall. Davey had already hit it once and he was pretty nervous about doing it again.

We walked to the very front of the ship and Mark went to the side next to the starboard side while I went to the port side. Davey had slowed the ship down to a crawl and the gates of the lock were open and waiting for us. We could see Davey moving the wheel a tiny bit from side to side as he watched the lock and the instruments. Captain McSorley was standing behind Davey calmly guiding him.

We were coming in from the lake and Davey had lined us up with the opening when a loud horn sounded from the lockmaster. Davey replied with one long toot and we moved ahead an inch at a time.

Mark was standing looking over the front of the boat and he watched as we came closer and closer to the cement wall. He put his hands up in the air about 4 feet apart, letting Davey know how close he was. We had about two feet on my side and I let Davey know by spacing my hands that far apart.

The ship moved farther into the lock and my space got wider. Mark was watching closely and had his hands about a foot apart. He looked up at Davey and shook his head. Davey corrected a bit but by the time he'd done it the ship had moved forward a few feet and was getting very close to the right wall.

Mark had his hands apart about six inches and then just used his finger and thumb to show the space. He was down to a couple of inches.

I braced for a collision. Mark crouched down like he was expecting a jolt. The ship moved forward and nothing happened. Mark began to grin and spread his hands apart to about a foot apart. I looked over the side and we had a good two feet on my side. I let Davey know and he adjusted the course.

We proceeded very slowly and made it the full length of the lock with not a scratch on either side. I looked up and Davey was grinning from ear to ear. Behind him Captain McSorley had a big smile on his face. He looked down at me and nodded.

We locked through and proceeded on toward Detroit.

Mark and I walked back toward the galley. Just as we passed the wheelhouse Davey came out of the door.

"Thanks for the help," he said.

"We'd rather do that than paint the bow again," Mark said.

Davey laughed and nodded. "You guys are the best," he said.

We made it to Detroit without any incidents and while the ship was unloaded we went to shore and had a fine time filling up on pizza and beer. We were scheduled to leave pretty early in the morning so we didn't overdo on the beer.

The next morning we were headed up toward Superior. Thomas came into the galley and snitched a cinnamon roll.

"The word is that we're going to make one more trip to Detroit next week and then that's it for the season," he said.

"The weather's still good, why just one more trip?" I asked.

"The weather can turn to crap really fast in November. If we get one more trip in without a storm we'll be lucky."

"So one more trip and then we're out of work," Mark said.

"Looks like that's about it," Thomas said.

"What day are we scheduled to leave?" I asked.

"November 9th," Thomas said.

"Cool," Mark said, "We'll be home for deer season."

We had no idea how wrong he was.

Chapter 47

By the time we had locked through and were back in Lake Superior it started raining. The sky was dark and low and it looked like evening even though it was just after noon. Mark and I cleaned up the galley after lunch and went to our quarters for a rest. After a nap we decided to walk up and see what Davey was doing. He was on the bridge so we took the under-deck walkway to the bow of the ship so we could stay out of the weather.

Davey was at the wheel and First Mate John was sitting at the control panel watching the dials. We talked with Davey a while and then John walked over to us.

"So I suppose you've heard, we've got one last trip this season," he said.

"Yeah, we heard that," I said.

"I figured you had. It seems like news travels fast aboard a ship. Have you heard this will probably be Captain McSorley's and my last trip?"

"No, we haven't heard. You're both retiring?"

John nodded. "We've sailed together for 30 years. We've been talking about spending more time with our families and are pretty much ready for some time ashore. The plan right now is to leave Superior on Nov. 9th and then deliver a load to Detroit. Then when we return, we're both finished."

"One last trip," I said. "It must be exciting to think of such a big change in your lives."

"Yes is it. I'm thinking of buying a little bait shop near my home. I'll sell a little bait, go fishing and maybe do a little sailing. I bought a sailboat a few years ago and I've only had it out three times."

"Well, I hope you have a great retirement," Mark said.

"Maybe they'll make me captain," Davey said grinning.

John looked at him and tried to suppress a grin. "Um,

maybe," he said.

We all laughed.

I could hear a sound like something was hitting the window and I turned toward the lake and saw it was sleeting.

"Yikes the weather is turning bad," I said.

"That stuff is sticking to the deck," Davey said. "It's going to be slippery out there."

"We're taking the under-deck walkway," Mark said. "In fact we better get back to the galley. We're having roast and mashed potatoes and Mike has to peel a bunch of potatoes."

I grinned at my twin. "Oh? Mike has to peel potatoes? Who decided that?"

Mark shrugged. "I thought I heard that you had volunteered to do it."

"Nice try," I said.

We said goodbye to Davey and John and left the bridge. The metal stairs leading down to the deck were solid ice.

"Hold on," I said to Mark.

"No kidding, a guy could bust his butt on this ice."

Mark had barely said that when my left foot flew out from under me just as I stepped onto the deck. I grabbed for the railing and lost my grip since it was covered with ice also. My left elbow slammed into the deck and my head hit the bottom step at the same time. I felt a huge bolt of pain shoot up my arm and then heard a bang inside my head. I knew I'd fallen but suddenly my ears began to ring and everything went black.

"Mike, Mike," Mark gently shook his brother. He was out cold and the back of his head was bleeding.

Mark ran up the stairs to the bridge and fell at the top step on the ice. He started sliding across the landing and if he hadn't grabbed the railing he would have slid off the landing and fallen to the deck below. He carefully got up and went inside.

"Mark fell on the ice," he said to John and Davey. "He's knocked out cold."

"I'll call for help," John said.

Mark made his way back down the slippery stairs and a minute later John came out on the landing. "Help is on the way," he said.

A short time later the door to the under-deck walkway opened and Thomas and Paul came running out. Paul's feet went out from under him and he fell on his backside and slid toward the edge of the deck. He grabbed a metal brace and stopped himself from going over the side.

"Damn, it's slick as hell up here," he said. "I almost went in the drink."

"What happened?" Thomas asked.

"We were coming down from the bridge and Mike slipped on the ice and hit his head. He's out cold."

"Let's carry him down to the walkway and get him back to sick bay."

Thomas picked up Mike's shoulders and Paul and Mark each took a foot and they managed to slip and slide their way across the deck and into the safety of the under-deck walkway. They carried him down the walkway for a little way and then had to lay him down.

"We need a stretcher," Paul said.

Paul ran to the stern of the ship where the medical sick bay was and returned with a stretcher a few minutes later. They put Mike on the stretcher and carried him the rest of the way. It was much easier going with the stretcher.

The ships medic had been summoned and he looked Mike over. His head was bleeding badly and he found a gash in his scalp.

"This isn't too bad. It looks worse than it is. A scalp wound bleeds like crazy but they usually aren't as bad as they seem. He took a shaver and shaved a spot off the back of Mike's head and revealed a small gash. He cleaned it off with alcohol and proceeded to stitch it up.

"It's a good thing he's out. This probably hurts a bit," he said.

Soon he had the wound stitched up and wrapped a gauze bandage around Mike's head making him look like a mummy.

"Okay, now we'll just keep an eye on him," he said.

"I'll stay," Thomas said. "I'm not on duty for a few hours."

Mark went to the galley to work and Paul went back to his job.

"I'll let you know when he wakes up," Thomas said as the rest of them left.

Chapter 48

When I woke up I had no idea where I was. The ceiling of the room I was in was different from that in my quarters. I raised my head and pain shot through it so I quickly lay back down. I must have moaned because I heard someone stir and when I opened my eyes again there was Thomas looking down at me.

"Hey, how are you feeling?" he asked.

"I feel like someone hit me in the head with a hammer," I replied, my voice hoarse.

"Well that's close," he said grinning. "You tried to remove the bottom step on the stairs leading up to the bridge with your head. You hit hard enough to knock yourself out."

I closed my eyes and tried to remember and had a fuzzy recollection of talking to Mark about how slippery the stairs were. I had no memory past that.

"Is it bad?" I asked.

"It bled a lot but the medic said you have a hard head and it will probably be okay. You've got a little bald spot on the back of your head where he stitched it up."

I lifted my right arm up and my head off the pillow and felt the gauze bandages surrounding my head.

"Cool, I'll get sympathy now," I said with a grin.

"Do you feel okay to sit up?" Thomas asked.

"Yeah, I think so," I replied.

Thomas took hold of my right arm and as I put weight on my left elbow a stabbing pain shot up my arm.

"Oh man!" I gasped. I lay back down and grimaced. "My elbow hurts like hell."

"Your elbow? I better call the medic. He didn't even look at your elbow. We thought you'd just hit your head."

Thomas hurried out of the sick bay and soon I heard him returning and the medic was with him.

"So you hit your elbow too?" he asked.

"I remember now that I hit it when I fell," I replied.

He carefully lifted my arm and felt around my elbow. He squeezed the elbow and pain shot up my arm. I gasped when he touched it.

"Did that hurt?" he asked.

"Damn right," I said grimacing.

He carefully laid my arm back on the cot.

"It might be broken. It feels like the radius bone might be shattered where it meets the upper arm. I can't do much but splint it. When we get ashore you'll have to go and get it x-rayed."

I nodded. "Thomas can you go and get Mark?"

Thomas left and the medic fitted a plastic blow-up splint on my elbow. He inflated it so it would be stabilized but not so much that it put a lot of pressure on the break.

"I'll give you a couple of Tylenol for now. I'm not allowed to give anything more potent but once you see a real doctor you'll probably get some "happy pills"."

I grinned at him. "Thanks, for helping," I said.

Mark came in looking a bit worried. "Thomas said you have a broken arm?"

I shrugged. "My elbow might be broken, I'm not going to be able to help much in the galley," I said.

"Don't worry about that. We can manage."

"We'll be in Duluth tomorrow morning," Thomas said. "Then we can get you to a doctor and get you fixed up."

"What about the last trip? I'm not going to be worth a crap for that."

"You're not much help anyway," Mark said laughing. "I've done most of the work all summer as it is."

"Oh bull," I said laughing.

"Let's see what they say about your elbow and then go from there. If it's broken you might as well stay in Chez-Dump and we'll take the last trip without you."

We agreed that was all we could do, so they went back to

work and I took a nap. Mark brought me dinner later and helped me eat it.

I felt well enough to sit up and after a while I went to the head and then back to our quarters. Mark and Davey joined me later and soon Paul and Thomas joined us.

My elbow hurt like heck and I was careful all night to keep it from touching anything. The night passed slowly and I got a little sleep now and then. As long as I lay still my elbow didn't ache too much but it seemed as soon as I slept, I'd move and make it hurt. I was glad to see morning shining in through our porthole.

We steamed into the dock and the crew tied up the ship. After everything was as it should be the five of us walked to the gangplank. Captain McSorley waved to us from the bridge and then came out the door.

"Good luck with the arm," he said.

"I'll let you know Sir. I hope to be able to make the final trip with you."

"If it's broken, just stay back and rest. We can make this last run without you. We'll be back in no time. But if you're well enough, you can come along. It's up to you."

Mark drove and we went to the hospital in Duluth. I went to the x-ray room while Mark filled out the paperwork. Once my arm was x-rayed it didn't take long to find out the end of the larger bone in my lower arm was broken off.

"See this little half–circle of bone?" the doctor said pointing to a little crescent shaped thing on the x-ray. "That should be attached to this bone here." He pointed at the long bone. "We can fix it by putting a thin screw into it and pinning it back to the bone but that will take surgery and a day in the hospital."

Well I didn't like the idea of that but I had no choice. So the doctor saw to it that I got to the right places for pre-operation preparation and Mark stayed with me. The others went back to the Dump.

That afternoon they took me into surgery and when I woke

up I had a cast on my elbow with my arm bent across my chest. I was a little groggy yet but glad to see my four friends standing at the side of my bed.

"So, how are you feeling?" Paul asked.

"Right now I feel great," I said.

"It's probably the morphine they gave you," Thomas said.

I nodded and grinned. "Good stuff," I said.

"Well take care and we'll come in the morning and get you," Davey said.

They left with the exception of Mark. "We talked to the doc and he said we can pick you up tomorrow. They like to keep you one night to make sure everything is okay."

I took his hand in my right hand. "Thanks for taking care of me."

"That's what brothers are for," he said.

"See you tomorrow," I said feeling warmth in my heart for my brother.

"Love ya bro."

Chapter 49

They had me hooked to a machine that allowed me to have a shot of morphine every half hour if I needed it. I didn't want to use it too much but for the first half of the evening I pushed the button quite a few times. Each time I'd feel nice and cozy and it didn't take long to see how people got addicted to something like that.

I finally slept long and hard about 1am and woke when a nurse came in to check my blood pressure and other vitals.

They brought me breakfast and I felt pretty good. My elbow hurt but it wasn't anything that was too awful. The doctor came in and checked me and said that my brother and friends were waiting to take me home.

They all came into my room and everyone was talking about me being so clumsy as I dressed. I had to put my tee shirt over my left arm because it was in a cast and I couldn't manage it through the sleeve hole. I had to ask for help buttoning my jeans much to my embarrassment.

"You want me to help with your jeans?"

I grinned at Mark, glad that he'd volunteered since he was my brother.

"You know we'll get shit from these guys."

Mark walked up and pulled my jeans up and buttoned the button and zipped me up.

"Oyvay," Davey said.

Everyone burst out laughing and Mark slugged Davey in the shoulder.

When we got back to Chez-Dump I sat in one of the good chairs and they waited on me pretty well for the rest of the day. Of course they decided they needed to have a few beers but I drank soda. The doc told me not to drink any alcohol with the meds I was taking or I might take a trip and never leave the farm.

Actually it was kind of fun to watch my friends as they got goofier and goofier as the night wore on. Davey was amusing us with tales of the sea. No one knew where he got the stories but they were pretty entertaining.

"So do you really think that this next trip to Detroit will be the captain's last one?" Mark asked.

Thomas shrugged. "He and John have sailed for many years together. They were together before they came on the *Fitzgerald*. I've heard they made a pact to sail together or go down to the bottom together."

"That's a cheery thought," Davey said.

"Well, they only have one trip left for the season. I suppose once they get back they'll decide one way or the other."

The next day we went to see Henry. He wasn't home so we drove over to the fishing dock and saw him sitting out on it fishing. He smiled as we all walked up but looked surprised when he saw my arm in a sling.

"What happened? Did you anger a young lady and she broke your arm?"

I laughed. "No nothing so exciting. I slipped on an icy deck and landed on my elbow and broke it."

"Ouch, so are you finished for the year?"

"I'm going to talk to Captain McSorley about it. We talked before I knew my arm was broken and he suggested I might want to stay behind. I'd like to make the last trip with the guys but I wouldn't be any help. I'm a lot more comfortable on shore where the floor stays in one place. This elbow is pretty tender."

"You might as well stay in the Dump and keep Tigger company," Mark said.

"We're going to Detroit and unload and turn right around and come back," Davey said. "The captain wants to get off the water as soon as possible. He said that November is not a good month to be out on Lake Superior."

"The captain is a smart man," Henry said. "The Chippewa always told stories of the lake and how dangerous it is in

November. Just imagine in their day when they traveled the lake in big canoes. I would not want to be on Lake Superior in a canoe, at any time of year, let alone November. It can go from calm to an unimaginable maelstrom in just a few hours."

I felt a chill when Henry said that. It was like the finger of death poked me.

Chapter 50

November 9, 1975

I rode with the guys down to the dock when they reported to the *Fitzgerald*. We had received instructions to be aboard by 1100 hours when we left a few days earlier. I wanted to talk to the captain so I rode along.

We parked the car and walked up the gangplank to the deck. Captain McSorley was on the bridge so I parted company with the others there as they went to their quarters to stow their gear.

"Well guys, have a safe trip," I said.

"You take care of yourself and try not to injure yourself any further," Thomas said grinning.

"We'll see you in a few days," Paul said slapping me on the back.

"Who's going to zip up your pants?" Davey smirked.

"Don't you worry about it," I said shoving him in the shoulder.

"Be safe guys," I said.

They all walked down the deck and disappeared through the deck door. Davey stopped and waved as he left the deck.

"Well, I guess you'll be okay till we get back," Mark said.

I nodded. "Tigger'll have to put up with me. I know she likes you better. I never figured out how she knew which of us was which."

"She has good taste," he said grinning.

"Well, I'll see ya then," he said. Then he stopped and hugged me.

"Be safe Mark," I whispered in his ear.

"I will," he said. Then he walked down the deck. I watched him go into the hatch. For some reason I felt like I should go and say something more to him, but I quickly shed that thought as just something a twin might do.

There were very few times in our lives where we'd been apart and this would be one where we'd not see each other for five or six days. Somehow it seemed wrong for me to leave.

I walked up the stairs and into the bridge. Captain McSorley was reading a chart and looked up at me.

"Well, I heard that you've been to the doctor," he said. "Is it true that your elbow is broken?"

"Yes Sir," I said. "I broke the end of the bone right off."

The captain shook his head. "I hope it's not too painful."

"I've got some pills that make it feel pretty good," I said.

"Well I suppose you're going to miss our last voyage," he said.

"I don't think I'd be of much use. The doctor said I should rest and let the elbow heal as long as I can so I think I'll be better off on shore. I hate to miss it."

"Oh don't worry, we're going to run down to Detroit, unload and turn right around. We shouldn't be gone very long at all. You take it easy and we'll see you in no time."

I shook hands with the captain and he walked me to the door. "Have a safe trip Sir," I said.

"Thank you Mike. We'll take good care of your brother."

I don't know what it was that made me feel so strange as I walked down the stairs and then down the gangplank. I looked to the northwest and there were big black storm clouds building on the horizon. It was going to be a rough voyage and I didn't think I'd miss all the tossing and turning that the ship was in for.

The wind had a distinct chill to it as I got into the car and drove back to the room. When I got there Tigger looked at me and then turned away and jumped up on the dresser and then to the top bunk and lay down.

I ate an apple and sat looking at the four walls thinking I was going to be really bored for the next few days.

"I'll go see Henry," I said to myself.

I walked down to the car and drove over to Henry's place. He was sitting in front looking at the now cloudy sky.

"A bad storm is coming," he said as I walked up his driveway.

"You think?" I said.

He nodded. "November is a bad month for storms. Some just go past and cause some rain. Some bring a big snowstorm. Others bring wind and big waves. November is not a good month on Lake Superior."

"The *Fitzgerald* is leaving for Detroit soon," I said.

"And you're not going?"

I shook my head. "I can't do anything with this broken arm. I'm suppose to take it easy."

Henry nodded. "Nobody should be going. I have a feeling this is going to be a big storm with lots of wind."

I sat in a chair next to Henry. "Would the captain stay in port if he thought it was too dangerous?"

"There's no way to know how bad it will be. These captains have a lot of experience. A guy like McSorley knows the lake. A ship like the *Fitzgerald* will stand more rough water than any other ship on the Great Lakes. I'm sure they'll be okay."

Somehow that didn't make me feel any less apprehensive.

Chapter 51

Aboard the *Edmund Fitzgerald*, the crew is busy putting the hatch covers on the now full ship. Twenty six thousand tons of taconite pellets have been loaded into the holds. At 2:20pm they cast off the lines and the ship steams out into the harbor.

On shore Henry and I watch the *Fitzgerald* steam down the harbor toward the lake. I stood up and walked to the end of the driveway looking to see if I can see anyone on the deck. I can see several deck hands tightening down the hatch bolts but can't tell who any of them are at this distance.

"Be safe Mark," I think.

"Don't worry," he answers back in our twin communication.

Aboard the *Edmund Fitzgerald* at 2:39pm the National Weather Service issues a gale warning for Lake Superior. The seas are running at 6 to 8 feet and they are having no problems. Aboard the *Arthur M. Anderson*, Captain Cooper radios the *Fitzgerald* that he has them on his radar. The two captains decide to keep in close contact since the weather is threatening.

Aboard the *Anderson* at 4:15pm, Captain Jesse Cooper radios that he is about 15 miles behind the *Fitzgerald*. Captain McSorley acknowledges this and continues on down the lake.

Aboard the *Wilfred Sykes*, Captain Dudley Paquette leaves Duluth harbor and takes a course that will afford them protection from some of the wind by steering close to Lake Superior's north shore. Captain Paquette is monitoring the radio and hears Captain McSorely aboard the *Fitzgerald* and Captain Cooper aboard the *Anderson* as they decide to take the regular course across the lake on their down-bound route.

On shore the weather deteriorated enough that Henry and I decided to move into his cottage. He invited me to stay for supper and I gladly accepted. Outside the storm increased. The wind was now blowing trash cans and signs down and scattering anything that wasn't heavy or nailed down all over the place. It began to rain just at dark.

"I bet you're glad you're here where the floor stays put," Henry said as he sat a plate of fresh northern fillets and potatoes on the table.

"Boy I guess. It's so hard trying to feed people when the ship is wallowing in those big waves. We spill as much as we eat," I said.

Henry nodded. "Let's say grace," he said. He reached over and took my good hand and we bowed our heads. "Heavenly Father we thank you for this fish that you have provided us from this wonderful lake you have created. Please keep our friends and brothers safe on the water tonight during their voyage. Amen."

"Amen," I said.

Henry had done an amazing job on the food as usual and even though I was uneasy about my brother and friends being out on the lake in such weather, I ate with gusto. When we finished Henry washed up while I sat and looked out the window into the darkness.

"They'll be okay," he said when he came back into the dining room.

"I know but it's got to be scary out there."

Henry nodded. "I'm sure it is."

As much as I hated to go out into the storm I thanked Henry and made a run for the car. I was soaked by the time I got the door open and sat dripping as I waited for the defroster to clear the windshield. I drove over to the room, ran up the stairs getting even more soaked and went into the Dump. Tigger looked up from her nest and meowed at me.

"Well, that's more than you usually say to me," I said. I

walked over and petted her head and she allowed it. Maybe I was making progress.

I stripped off my wet clothes and hung them up to dry. I slipped on a pair of sweatpants that didn't need to be zipped up and a sweatshirt and lay down on one of the bunks and tried to sleep.

November 10, 1975

Aboard the *Edmund Fitzgerald* at 1:00am Captain McSorley radios that they are 20 miles south of Isle Royale. The wind is blowing at 52 knots, which translated to about 56 miles per hour. Waves have built to 10 feet.

Mark and the others are all sleeping uneasily in their quarters. The ship is tossing and turning and it makes it very hard to do anything let alone get some good rest.

"Mark, are you sleeping?" Davey asked quietly.

"No, just when I doze off I get slammed and wake up again."

"It's getting bad."

"Do you think we're going to be okay?"

"I think the captain knows what to do. If it gets too bad he'll head for Whitefish Bay. We can get some shelter there. At least that's what I'd do."

"Well, try to sleep," Mark said.

Chapter 52

Aboard the *Edmund Fitzgerald* at 2am, the weather service upgrades the storm warning to gale force winds of 35-50 knots. The *Anderson* had been following the *Fitzgerald* but being a faster ship they pull ahead of the other ship. At 2:45am it begins snowing. The *Anderson* looses sight of the *Fitzgerald* in the blizzard.

Aboard the *Wlfred Sykes* Captain Paquette hears Captain McSorley radio to the *Anderson* that he is slowing and that they were going to try for some lee from Isle Royale.

At the Dump I have lain awake most of the night. The wind is howling outside and every now and then a huge gust slams against the building actually making the whole house shake. Finally I decided to get up and sit in one of the big soft chairs and try to sleep. I moved the chair over in front of the window and pulled up a footstool in front of it. I pulled a blanket off the bed and wrapped up in the blanket.

The streetlight was swinging with the wind making strange shadows on the street. Every now and then something would fly past, a trashcan, a lawn chair, and once a kid's swimming pool went flying by.

The harbor looked angry and dangerous. Though there was land that sheltered it from the wind, there were six-foot waves running down the length of it. Sailboats rocked and their rigging rang against their metal masts. Waves crashed against the sea walls and piers.

Tigger jumped up onto the windowsill and looked out at the lake. She began to meow mournfully. I reached over and picked her up and she allowed me to lay her on my chest. She looked into my eyes and meowed sadly.

"What's wrong little girl?" I whispered.

She curled up and lay on my chest and looked toward the window.

"Mark are you awake?"

His voice didn't come into my head like it usually did. I wasn't sure if he could "hear" me when he was so far away. We'd always been close to each other when we communicated without speaking before.

"It's bad out here Mike."

"Are you safe?"

"So far... the waves are huge, we're all in our quarters, Thomas, Paul, Davey and me."

"I wish I was there."

"No you don't want to be here. The captain ordered everyone off the deck. We're in trouble Mike."

I began to pray.

Aboard the *Edmund Fitzgerald* at 7am: The captain reports that the winds are at a sustained 35 knots and the seas are running at 10 feet. They are near Caribou Island and rounding the island near Six Fathom Shoal.

Aboard the *Arthur Anderson,* Captain Cooper reports that he is watching the *Fitzgerald* and it seems much too close to Six Fathom Shoal. "I would not want to be that close," he reports.

At the Dump I am waking up after finally falling asleep. Tigger is curled on my chest sleeping soundly and wakes up as I move. She looks out the window and meows. Then she jumps off my chest and down to the floor and off to her litter box. Outside the storm still rages. The rain comes in sheets slamming against the side of the house. Then minutes later the rain turns to sleet and then to snow. Even though the harbor is close by I can barely see the water. I shudder as I think of being out on the lake in this weather.

Aboard the *Edmund Fitzgerald* at 3:30pm: Captain McSorley radios Captain Cooper aboard the *Arthur Anderson*:

McSorley: *"Anderson,* this is *Fitzgerald.* I have sustained some topside damage. I have a fence rail laid down. Two vents lost or damaged and a list. I am checking down. Will you stay with me to Whitefish?"

Cooper: "*Fitzgerald*, do you have your pumps going?"

McSorley: "Yes both of them."

McSorley advised the *Anderson* that he was going to slow his ship down so the *Anderson* could close the gap between them. The Coast Guard broadcast a warning that all the Soo Locks had been closed and all ships should seek safe anchorage.

Aboard the *Edmmund Fitzgerald* at 4:10pm, Captain McSorley radios the *Anderson* that he has a radar failure and asks the *Anderson* to keep track of them. The *Fitzgerald* is effectively blind and has slowed so the *Anderson* can catch up to them. The *Anderson* closes within 10 miles of the other ship.

McSorley: "*Anderson* this is the *Fitzgerald*. I have lost both radars. Can you provide me with radar plots until we reach Whitefish Bay?"

Cooper: "Charlie on that *Fitzgerald*. We'll keep you advised of position."

At the Dump I'm settled into the chair in front of the window with Tigger in my lap. Even though I can't do a thing to help, I feel closer to my brother and my friends looking out the window toward the lake where they are struggling.

"Mike, it's getting worse."

"What's happened?"

"We're listing to the port side. When we look out the porthole in our cabin the water is just below it."

I was shocked. That porthole was usually fifteen feet above the water line.

"Are they using the pumps?"

"Yeah, Thomas says they should catch up soon."

"How are you guys doing?"

"We're scared Mike… we're scared to death."

Chapter 53

Aboard the *Edmund Fitzgerald* the captain realizes that he cannot pick up the Whitefish Point radio beacon. He radios the Coast Guard on the emergency channel.

McSorley: "Coast Guard, can you confirm that the beacon and light at Whitefish Point are operational?"

Coast Guard: "Our monitoring equipment shows that both instruments are inactive."

McSorley: "Any ship, any ship in the Whitefish Point area, can anyone confirm the light and beacon are operational? Any ship, any ship, confirm Whitefish Point radio beacon and light are operational?"

Captain Cedric Woodard, aboard the *Avafors*: "We can confirm the light is on but not the radio beacon."

Captain Woodard waited for an answer. A transmission came a few seconds later:

"Don't allow nobody on deck." Transmission garbled. "a vent."

Woodard: "The wind is really howling down here. What are the conditions where you are?"

McSorley" "I have a bad list, lost both radars and am taking heavy seas over the deck. This is one of the worst seas I have ever been in."

Woodard: "If I am correct you have two radars."

McSorley: "They're both gone."

Aboard the *Arthur Anderson*, at 7pm the ship is struck by two huge waves that push water across the deck of the ship. The deck is normally 35 feet above the water line. The waves hit with so much force that they damage one of the lifeboats secured to the deck.

At the Dump Tigger and I are sitting at the window watching

as the storm rages. The winds seem to be building. They have switched direction from northeast to south and then back to northeast. It is dark and the streets are deserted at the early hour of 7pm.

"Mike we're having a hell of a time."

"What's happened?"

"The list is worse. Our porthole is under water. We're nearly standing on the wall of the room. We're scared Mike."

"Can you get to a lifeboat?"

"It would be suicide. The waves are as high as the ship."

"Oh God Mark, hang on, please hang on."

"We're all together. Thomas and Paul are here with Davey and me yet. We're going to stay together to the end."

"Don't say that... do not say that!"

"Pray for us Mike."

Aboard the *Arthur Anderson*, at 7:10pm captain Cooper calls the *Fitzgerald*.

Cooper: *"Fitzgerald* this is the *Anderson.* Have you checked down?"

McSorley: "Yes we have."

Cooper: *"Fitzgerald*, we are about 10 miles behind you and gaining about 1 ½ miles per hour. *Fitzgerald* there is a target 19 miles ahead of us. So the target would be 9 miles ahead of you."

McSorley: "Well, am I going to clear?"

Cooper: "Yes. He is going to pass to the west of you."

McSorley: Well, fine."

Cooper: "By the way *Fitzgerald*, how are you making out with your problem?"

McSorley: "We are holding our own."

At the Dump Tigger and I are still watching the storm rage outside the window, rain splattering against the glass and trees are whipping and lashing. I look at my watch: it is 7:20pm.

"Mike something has happened!"

"Mark, what's going on?"

"Mike, we're going over. There was a huge bang and... I think we're going down Mike!"
"Mark! Mark talk to me."
"Thomas thinks the ship has broken in half. Oh God, oh God."
"Mark... Mark."
"There's water, water coming in, the hall is flooded the room is filling up. Cold, cold Mike."
"Mark!"
"It's so cold. The lights have gone out. It's dark, and cold. Oh God Mike, we're sinking! Tell mom and dad I love them. I love you Mike."
"Mark... I love you too..."

I can barely breathe. My heart is pounding and my head is spinning. I've just heard my brother die. Tigger is sitting in the window and is meowing sadly as if she knows what I have just learned. My brother and my friends are gone. The captain and all of the friends I've made on the ship are gone. I close my eyes and cry.

Aboard the *Arthur Anderson* at 7:20pm the mate manning the radar looks up to Captain Cooper with an amazed expression.
"It's gone," he says.
"What's gone?"
"The *Fitzgerald* Sir, it's gone. One minute it was right there on the radar and the next it disappeared."
Captain Cooper picks up the microphone.
"*Arthur Anderson* calling the *Edmund Fitzgerald*, come in please." "*Fitzgerald*, do you read me?" "This is the *Anderson* calling the *Fitzgerald*, do you read?"
Captain Cooper stares out at the raging sea.
"Coast Guard, Coast Guard, this is the *Arthur M. Anderson*. We have lost contact with the *Edmund Fitzgerald* and I fear she has gone down."

Chapter 54

I sat in stunned silence in the dark room. Tigger lay on my lap meowing quietly. I picked her up and stroked her fur.

"You know somehow don't you?" I said.

I didn't understand it but somehow the little cat knew the rest of her people were never coming back.

I was exhausted. My twin brother who I'd spent nearly every waking minute for the last 20 years was gone forever. I wondered how long it would be before the authorities let the news out that the *Fitzgerald* was lost. I needed to call my parents and let them know that Mark was gone but I was safe. Otherwise they'd think they'd lost both of their sons. I made the hardest call of my life.

My parents were devastated but glad I had not been aboard when the ship went down. At first my dad thought maybe I'd just dreamed my "conversation" with Mark but he knew. He'd seen us communicate without words many times. I told them I'd be home in a few days and said goodbye after a long tearful call. Then I lay down on the bed. Exhaustion overtook me and I slept deeply.

The next morning I woke to sunshine coming in through the front window. Tigger was lying in a sunbeam sleeping. I got up and looked out to a nice morning with a slight breeze. The lake was calm and everything looked like nothing out of the ordinary had happened.

As I turned to get dressed I looked down and there was Henry standing on the sidewalk in front of the house looking up at our room. I opened the window and motioned for him to come up.

I met Henry at the porch and his eyes were red and he looked pale and very frail.

"Have you heard?" he said.

"I know," I said. "I was with them when they were lost. Mark communicated with me."

Henry looked confused. "How did he communicate with you?"

"It's something we've always done. I can hear his voice in my head and he can hear mine. They were all together. Mark and Thomas and Paul and Davey were all together. They were frightened but it happened very quickly. They didn't suffer."

"The radio said all hands were lost."

"I was never an official member of the crew. Mark and I filled one job. That was all they had left when we were hired. Mark filled out the papers and I just went along for the ride. We shared the work but only he got paid. We were there for the experience of seeing how a ship worked. So officially I was never a member of the crew."

"So no one will ever know that one person survived," Henry said.

"Yeah, I guess so."

"So what will you do now?"

"I'm going to pack up Mark's and my things and go home. I'll go back to school in January and hopefully graduate in a year."

"I never expected something like this," Henry said. "The five of you have become kind of like grandsons to me. I never thought I'd outlive four of you."

I hugged Henry. "The guys all loved you Henry. They really enjoyed their time with you. We often talked of you like an extra grandpa."

His eyes filled with tears and he walked out on the porch for a few minutes and then he returned.

"Do you want some help packing up?" he asked.

"Sure, that'd be great," I said.

I went down to the liquor store and got some empty boxes. The man who ran it was surprised when I walked in so I had to explain to him how I missed being on the ship. He was very sad to hear that the rest of the guys were gone.

Henry and I packed each of the other's things in boxes, taped them up and wrote their names on the boxes so their relatives could pick their stuff up later. I found the package of pictures I'd taken aboard the *Fitzgerald*. Mark had gotten them developed. We looked through them. I had to smile at my friends and the captain and the pictures of the great ship. These pictures were precious to me. The last thing I picked up was the picture of Mark and I on the first day we looked out over Lake Superior.

"We were so excited that day," I said showing the picture to Henry. "We had the world at our feet and were embarking on a new adventure. We never would have thought that it would end like this." Henry looked at the picture and his eyes filled with tears.

"You keep that," I said. He nodded and hugged me.

When everything was packed up all that remained was Tigger. The little cat looked around at all the boxes and seemed to know that something was not going to be the same. She came to me and looked up and meowed.

I bent down and picked her up. "What's wrong little girl? Are you afraid we'll just leave you behind?"

She rubbed her face on my chest and purred.

"I think she wants to go with you," Henry said.

I nodded. "I think so too. I'll take her home with me. She'll have a home as long as she needs one."

We carried my stuff down to the car and then I went back up and got the cat. I put her into the front seat. She curled up in my sweatshirt that was lying on the seat and looked like she was ready for a nap. I turned to Henry. I hugged the old man and we both had tears in our eyes.

"Have a long life," he said to me. "I'll miss all of you. These past months have been wonderful for an old man who is always alone. You guys made me feel young again."

"Thanks for everything Henry. All of the guys loved you like a grandfather. You made all of our lives better."

Henry smiled a very sad smile and turned and walked away. My heart ached for the old man.

I crossed the bridge into Wisconsin and when I got to the top of the hill I stopped at the lookout point by the lighthouse where Mark and I had stopped for the picture at the beginning of the summer. I picked up Tigger and carried her over to the rock wall and we looked out across the huge expanse of water. Somewhere out there my brother and my friends were entombed in the *Edmund Fitzgerald*. Tigger meowed and put her face next to my neck.

"Farewell my friends," I said. "Till we meet again."

I got in the car and drove toward home, and never saw Lake Superior again.

The Wreck of the Edmund Fitzgerald

by

Gordon Lightfoot

The legend lives on from the Chippewa on down
Of the big lake they called 'Gitche Gumee'
The lake, it is said, never gives up her dead
When the skies of November turn gloomy
With a load of iron ore twenty-six thousand tons more
Than the Edmund Fitzgerald weighed empty.
That good ship and crew was a bone to be chewed
When the gales of November came early.

The ship was the pride of the American side
Coming back from some mill in Wisconsin
As the big freighters go, it was bigger than most
With a crew and good captain well seasoned
Concluding some terms with a couple of steel firms
When they left fully loaded for Cleveland
And later that night when the ship's bell rang
Could it be the north wind they'd been feelin'?

The wind in the wires made a tattletale sound
And a wave broke over the railing
And every man knew, as the captain did too,
T'was the witch of November come stealin'.
The dawn came late and the breakfast had to wait
When the Gales of November came slashin'.
When afternoon came it was freezin' rain
In the face of a hurricane west wind.

When suppertime came, the old cook came on deck sayin'.
Fellas, it's too rough to feed ya.
At Seven P.M. a main hatchway caved in, he said
Fellas, it's been good t'know ya
The captain wired in he had water comin' in
And the good ship and crew was in peril.
And later that night when his lights went outta sight
Came the wreck of the Edmund Fitzgerald.

Does any one know where the love of God goes
When the waves turn the minutes to hours?
The searchers all say they'd have made Whitefish Bay
If they'd put fifteen more miles behind her.
They might have split up or they might have capsized;
May have broke deep and took water.
And all that remains is the faces and the names
Of the wives and the sons and the daughters.

Lake Huron rolls, Superior sings
In the rooms of her ice-water mansion.
Old Michigan steams like a young man's dreams;
The islands and bays are for sportsmen.
And farther below Lake Ontario
Takes in what Lake Erie can send her,
And the iron boats go as the mariners all know
With the Gales of November remembered.

In a musty old hall in Detroit they prayed,
In the Maritime Sailors' Cathedral.
The church bell chimed till it rang twenty-nine times
For each man on the Edmund Fitzgerald.
The legend lives on from the Chippewa on down
Of the big lake they call 'Gitche Gumee'.
Superior, they said, never gives up her dead
When the gales of November come early!

Edmund Fitzgerald Facts

The *Edmund Fitzgerald* lies in 530 feet of water about 17 miles from the entrance to Whitefish Bay. The ship broke in half and the bow section is nearly 276 in length and sits upright in the mud, some 170 feet from the stern section. The stern section measures 253 feet in length and lies face down at a fifty-degree angle from the bow. The midsection of the ship has been reduced to rubble and heaps of taconite ore.

There are some liberties taken with actual timelines in this book. To make the story workable I had to condense the life of the ship to one summer when it came to incidents like hitting the lock wall and hitting another ship. These things happened but not all in that fatal summer.

I used the first names of real crew members for my characters. I make no assertions to the real nature of any of them. The young men in my story did what young men of that time did when it came to having fun and recreation. They worked hard at their jobs and when they had down time I'm sure they played hard too. The wreck has fascinated me since that day in November 1975 when I saw the first story in a newspaper about it. I wrote this story as a tribute to the crew and officers of the ship. While I had no knowledge of any of them personally, I felt it put a human face on the tragedy to delve into the lives of some of them. The use of a twin is a vehicle so the story can be told from the vantage point of someone who was there. The crew of 29 men who perished that fatal day should be remembered as sons, brothers, fathers and grandfathers and as brave sailors who died while doing their job on a great ship on one of the largest lakes in the world.

Crew of the *Edmund Fitzgerald*

(Name, Age, Occupation Onboard, Hometown)

Michael E. Armagost, 37, Third Mate, Iron River, Wisconsin

Fred J. Beetcher, 56, Porter, Superior, Wisconsin

Thomas D. Bentsen, 23, Oiler, St. Joseph, Michigan

Edward F. Bindon, 47, First Asst. Engineer, Fairport Harbor, Ohio

Thomas D. Borgeson, 41, Maintenance Man, Duluth, Minnesota

Oliver J. Champeau, 41, Third Asst. Engineer, Sturgeon Bay, Wisconsin

Nolan S. Church, 55, Porter, Silver Bay, Minnesota

Ransom E. Cundy, 53, Watchman, Superior, Wisconsin

Thomas E. Edwards, 50, Second Asst. Engineer, Oregon, Ohio

Russell G. Haskell, 40, Second Asst. Engineer, Millbury, Ohio

George J. Holl, 60, Chief Engineer, Cabot, Pennsylvania

Bruce L. Hudson, 22, Deck Hand, North Olmsted, Ohio

Allen G. Kalmon, 43, Second Cook, Washburn, Wisconsin

Gordon F. MacLellan, 30, Wiper, Clearwater, Florida

Joseph W. Mazes, 59, Special Maintenance, Ashland, Wisconsin

John H. McCarthy, 62, First Mate, Bay Village, Ohio

Ernest M. McSorley, 63, Captain, Toledo, Ohio

Eugene W. O'Brien, 50, Wheelsman, Toledo, Ohio

Karl A. Peckol, 20, Watchman, Ashtabula, Ohio

John J. Poviach,59, Wheelsman, Bradenton, Florida

James A. Pratt, 44, Second Mate, Lakewood, Ohio

Robert C. Rafferty, 62, Steward, Toledo, Ohio

Paul M. Riippa, 22, Deck Hand, Ashtabula, Ohio

John D. Simmons, 63, Wheelsman, Ashland, Wisconsin

William J. Spengler, 59, Watchman, Toledo, Ohio

Mark A. Thomas, 21, Deck Hand, Richmond Heights, Ohio

Ralph G. Walton, 58, Oiler, Fremont, Ohio

David E. Weiss, 22, Cadet, Agoura, California

Blaine H. Wilhelm, 52, Oiler, Moquah, Wisconsin

ABOUT THE AUTHOR

Dan Bomkamp has made his home in the Wisconsin River valley all his life with the exception of his college years in La Crosse. He has been an avid hunter and fisherman his whole life. For many years he was in the sporting goods industry and began writing in the 80s for outdoor magazines. He is active in the Foreign Exchange Student program having hosted 33 boys from 13 countries over the years. Golden Retrievers have also been a big part of his life. He had at least one Golden sharing his home for 33 years. He lives in Muscoda with his cat, Tigger and his Boston Terrier, Buster.

Check out his website at www.danbomkamp.com

Or you can email him: danbomkamp@live.com